YOU'RE GOING TO BE WHAT?!

You know how people say that some folks can't walk and chew gum at the same time? Oh yeah, they were talking about me.

I fall down stairs and roll out of bed onto the floor. I drop things on my toes and get trapped in closets. I've broken my arm making cookies. Don't ask. I even got locked in my own locker once.

Do you know how embarrassing it is to be caught in a locker?

Just ask me.

But a while ago everything changed because of something I saw on the Folk Arts Channel.

Yes, ladies and gentlemen, boys and girls, people I've run over, stepped on, and tripped up . . . I am going to be a square dance star.

And not only am I going to be a star, I'm going to be the fifth-grade school gym square dance champ of the whole world. And nobody's going to stop me. . . .

OTHER BOOKS YOU MAY ENJOY

TRIPPING OVER THE LUNCH LADY

AND OTHER SCHOOL STORIES

EDITED BY **NANCY E. MERCADO**

PUFFIN BOOKS

PUFFIN BOOKS
Published by the Penguin Group
Penguin Young Readers Group,
345 Hudson Street, New York, New York 10014, U.S.A.
Penguin Group (Canada), 90 Eglinton Avenue East, Suite 700, Toronto, Ontario,
Canada M4P 2Y3 (a division of Pearson Penguin Canada Inc.)
Penguin Books Ltd, 80 Strand, London WC2R 0RL, England
Penguin Ireland, 25 St Stephen's Green, Dublin 2, Ireland
(a division of Penguin Books Ltd)
Penguin Group (Australia), 250 Camberwell Road, Camberwell, Victoria 3124, Australia
(a division of Pearson Australia Group Pty Ltd)
Penguin Books India Pvt Ltd, 11 Community Centre, Panchsheel Park,
New Delhi - 110 017, India
Penguin Group (NZ), Cnr Airborne and Rosedale Roads, Albany, Auckland 1310,
New Zealand (a division of Pearson New Zealand Ltd)
Penguin Books (South Africa) (Pty) Ltd, 24 Sturdee Avenue, Rosebank,
Johannesburg 2196, South Africa

Registered Offices: Penguin Books Ltd, 80 Strand, London WC2R 0RL, England

First published in the United States of America by Dial Books,
a member of Penguin Group (USA) Inc., 2004
Published by Puffin Books, a division of Penguin Young Readers Group, 2006

10 9 8 7 6 5 4

"Tripping Over the Lunch Lady" © Angela Johnson, 2004
"How I got my english A" © Avi, 2004
"Experts, Incorporated" © Sarah Weeks, 2004
"Apple Blossoms" © Terry Trueman, 2004
"Science Friction" © David Lubar, 2004
"The Grade School Zone" © James Proimos, 2004
"The Desk" © Lee Wardlaw Jaffurs, 2004
"The Crush" © Rachel Vail, 2004
"The Girls' Room" © Susan Shreve, 2004
"Tied to Zelda" © David Rice, 2004

THE LIBRARY OF CONGRESS HAS CATALOGED THE DIAL BOOKS EDITION AS FOLLOWS:
Tripping over the lunch lady : and other school stories
edited by Nancy E. Mercado.
p.   cm.
Summary: An anthology of ten humorous short stories about life in school, written by
well-known authors of children's books.
ISBN 0-8037-2873-5 (hc)

1. Schools—Juvenile fiction. 2. Children's stories, American. [1. Schools—Fiction.
2. Short stories. 3. Humorous stories.] I. Mercado, Nancy E., date. II. Title.
PZ5.T776 2004   [Fic]—dc22   2003015905

Puffin Books ISBN 0-14-240624-4

Printed in the United States of America

CONTENTS

TRIPPING OVER THE LUNCH LADY

AND OTHER SCHOOL STORIES

INTRODUCTION

What do I remember most about school?

Watching a boy shoot chocolate milk out of his nose...

Throwing up from a bad batch of sloppy joes...

Sneak-reading books during boring assemblies...

Making the coolest medieval village out of cardboard for a fair that we never even entered...

Feeling left out...

Winning the game for my kickball team (I think I might be making this one up...I'm not sure!)...

Leaving other kids out...

Playing run-catch-and-kiss in the school yard...

Falling in love with whatever boy happened to sit next to me...

Getting yelled at by my English teacher for applying nail polish in class ("Do you see me *brushing my teeth* in class, Miss Mercado??")...

Singing mean songs about the bus driver on the bus ride home...

Kicking a girl in the eye by accident while doing a spazzy cartwheel in gym...

And the list could go on and on and on . . .

My school years were fun, exciting, and, I daresay, even magical at times, but I gotta face facts . . . they also had their share of terrible and terrifying things that felt like they were the absolute end of the world.

All of the authors in this collection have had their share of good and bad school experiences as well. And some of them have woven those experiences and/or feelings about school into fictional short stories. You might find that these stories are pretty funny. (I did.) And yet many of these stories involve something potentially painful. Having a crush, speaking in front of the class, struggling to keep up with everyone else, being the new kid, etc. To me, the best thing about all of these stories is how they use humor to explore these tricky situations.

Adults often say "You'll laugh about this later!" and how annoying is that? But I think the point is that humor and pain sometimes go together. It's why we laugh when we fall flat on our faces and it's why the crazy and awful things later on make *the best* stories. After all, who really wants to hear a story about the kid who got all A's and was enormously liked by everyone? I know I don't.

I am pleased to say that we have ten of the best storytellers gathered together in this collection. Avi, Angela Johnson, David Lubar, James Proimos, David Rice, Susan Shreve, Terry Trueman, Rachel Vail, Lee Wardlaw, and Sarah Weeks have all contributed great stories that make me laugh out loud and remind me of what school was truly like. I hope you'll enjoy them as much as I did.

Yours till the bell doesn't ring,

Nancy M.

Nancy E. Mercado

TRIPPING OVER THE LUNCH LADY

by Angela Johnson

I'm never going to be a gymnast.

You know how people say that some folks can't walk and chew gum at the same time? Oh yeah, they were talking about me.

I fall down stairs and roll out of bed onto the floor. I drop things on my toes and get trapped in closets. I've broken my arm making cookies. Don't ask. I even got locked in my own locker once. I wanted to see what it was like inside, and had to stay there till the end of school for the janitor to let me out.

Do you know how embarrassing it is to be caught in a locker?

Just ask me.

I'm especially not good with my feet *off* the ground. I was telling Mr. Deimeister just that, about the time I went flying off the trampoline over Tony Friedman's head yesterday and scared him so bad (he wasn't spotting for me but was talking to Gus Jackson about what they were going to do after school) that he choked on some gum he wasn't supposed to have in his mouth.

Right around the time he was having the Heimlich done on him and Gus was screaming to apply direct pressure (luckily we'd just had a first-aid class the period before gym), I realized that what everybody calls me is probably true.

Jinx.

That's how everyone refers to me. My own parents, even.

Mom thinks it's cute. My uncle Jeff began calling me Jinx when I started crawling backward as a baby and getting stuck in boxes, under tables, and even, the story goes, a pair of my dad's boots.

Dad pats me on the head like an old skunky stray and says Uncle Jeff was just like me.

Yeah, right.

Uncle Jeff drives a Porsche and lives in a cabin in the woods with a hot tub.

I'm too uncoordinated to ever drive a car and I'm

pretty sure a hot tub is just a bad accident waiting to happen. I love Uncle Jeff anyway, though. I guess he might have been a jinx back in the day. But hey, he must have grown out of it, which doesn't necessarily mean I will.

I'm never going to be able to keep my feet together and fly perfectly on the trampoline. I'm never going to be able to make a basket without breaking somebody's bones (the doctors did do a good job on Mr. Deimeister's nose, though). I'm never going to run like my sister or kick a soccer ball like my brother without falling, throwing up, or pulling a muscle on me or somebody else. My dad won't even let me use a steak knife. I still have to cut meat with one of those plastic picnic things that sort of look like a knife.

But a while ago everything changed—my whole life, even, because of something I saw on the Folk Arts Channel. A couple days after that, a picture in an album made it feel exactly right.

Yes, ladies and gentlemen, boys and girls, people I've run over, stepped on, and tripped up . . . I am going to be a square dance star.

The dancers on television floated over the floor,

arm in arm. They smiled, laughed, and nobody fell into anybody else or sprained anything. They were all so happy and even seemed to really like each other. And then I saw this woman who looked just like my mom. She could have been my mom, she looked so much like her. Then in the middle of a swing around she looked the camera in the eye and smiled at me. Honest, it was as if she looked right at me to say: "You could be me, and look—I can do this."

Wow.

It was a couple of days later when a picture fell out of a photo album I'd just dropped in the fish tank (I rescued everything pretty quick, except now our goldfish hide when I come close to the tank), but there in living color was a picture of my mom arm in arm with this kid with hair way down his back—square dancing.

It was in my genes.

I knew then it was meant to be.

And not only am I going to be a star, I'm going to be the fifth-grade school gym square dance champ of the whole world. And nobody's going to stop me—ouch . . .

It's a hard thing to change people's minds about how things are done and to get them to do something new.

This is how it went with Mr. Deimeister when I went to his office and told him what might be the most wonderful thing since kneepads and bandages.

"What?" he said, sort of backing away from me like he always does.

"Square dancing, Mr. Deimeister. Square dancing. It's fun and it's good exercise for everybody. I saw it on the Folk Arts Channel and practiced with a huge stuffed teddy bear."

"What?"

"It was real cool the way the guys swung the girls and everybody skipped and twirled around the room. I think it would be good for us all to learn a new skill, learn to dance with partners ('cause usually the boys don't want to), and get a good workout."

"What?"

"We wouldn't have to wear the frilly dresses or bow ties like they did on TV. I think our regular gym clothes would be okay. Do you think they have square dance music in the band room?"

"What?"

I think a few more meetings with Mr. Deimeister will get him to come around to the square dance way. So later that day I dropped off some square dance music at his office. He wasn't there and I accidentally dropped a ten-pound weight I was moving off his desk onto a fishing pole that fell on the floor. There was a stuffed fish over his desk.

Scary.

I thought we'd be dancing by now, but days after my meeting with Mr. Deimeister we're still on the trampoline that decided a long time ago it didn't like me. Evil is what it is. Evil. And it won't even take pity on my poor classmates, who have to keep catching me and throwing me back on it.

Mr. Deimeister keeps yelling, "Spot Jinx, spot Jinx!"

I'm feeling like a clumsy Dalmatian with all the spot Jinx going on. And I'm thinking how happy I'd be if my two feet were safely planted on the wooden floor, promenading down the court. Square dancing would save me.

I'd be the world's best square dancer. Maybe I could even stop wars and hunger with square dancing. I'd go to other countries and dance with my square dance group that would not include any of the people who back away when I use a fork in the lunchroom or have their arms stretched out to catch me when I'm going down the stairs to art class.

Maybe I'd get some award for ending unhappiness in the world by spreading square dance love all over the planet.

Maybe I'd change the whole wide wor—

"*Spot Jinx!*"

And maybe I'll do that after I come back from the nurse's office.

"I don't really want to square dance, Jinx."

Victoria is my best friend and I was counting on her to help me in the gym square dance campaign. Anyway, she's a good dancer and hasn't broken Mr. Deimeister's nose.

"C'mon, Vic. You have to be with me on this. I'm sick of dodge ball and volleyball. I broke half the gym windows and knocked out two people before Mr. Deimeister sat me on the bench to watch the clock."

"I still don't want to square dance, Jinx. We'll look stupid. The boys won't do it and all the girls will end up dancing together with the boys laughing at us."

Victoria pulls her braids back and blows a big bubble. Señora Smith comes over and taps her on the shoulder.

"No gum in Spanish class. How can you learn a new language with Super Bubble in your mouth?"

When Vic swallows the gum, Señora Smith makes a face and goes back to teaching us how to ask for a bathroom in Spanish.

"So what if they laugh. It'll be fun. Our feet will be on the ground and there won't be any round hard balls to knock anybody down or break anything. Help me out. This could be great.

My best friend forever, Vic will be.

She's going to the gym during our free period to practice with me.

We'll be square dance champions of the world when we finish.

Square dancing forever.

回∫回

I'll be carrying Vic's books for a few weeks to class for her.

Her foot cast is pretty cool, though. Bright purple and she let me draw orange daisies all over it already. Everybody is so nosy in this school. Within minutes everyone knew that we were square dancing under the basketball hoop when the broken foot thing happened. You'd pretty much think that would change my mind about square dancing, except technically it was Vic's fault.

We were doing just fine until she thought she heard people coming through the gym doors and turned to run.

Her feet got twisted up with mine. I still feel bad for her, though.

Oh, to be a square dancer.

But I've got a plan.

I printed out five hundred flyers that say SQUARE DANCE MANIA and taped them up all over the school to get people talking. But the next day everybody just looked confused when they read them, including Mr. Deimeister, who just shook his head and stared at me. And it didn't do anything to keep my feet from flying underneath me and the trampoline from smacking me in the face.

I'm so used to trampoline face by now.

I dreamed last night that all of Warren Harding Elementary School was square dancing through the streets. Everybody swung their partners do-si-do. Allemande right to the corners, then we all joined hands and circled to the left.

When I woke up, I was lying on the floor with a sore arm, probably from swinging my partners in my sleep. I guess my dreams of being a gym class hero in square dancing are pretty much squashed since now the whole school knows how Vic's foot got broken.

I spend the whole gym class with all of my friends and enemies skipping around me until Mr. Deimeister says, "The next person to skip around Jinx is running one hundred laps."

Bounce,
bounce,
bounce,
on the evil trampoline.

My mom says to give it up.

My dad just laughs.

My little sister sticks her tongue out at me and calls me doofus.

So I've been thinking, just thinking maybe, maybe square dancing isn't the thing. Maybe I can bring peace to the world and less bruises to myself with something else. Maybe jumping rope or jacks in gym might be okay....

But then, in gym, Mr. Deimeister says he wants to see me after class.

What's that about? It's been a couple of days since I hurt anybody, and the nurse even stopped me in the hall today to ask if I've been absent.

Anyway in the end I don't get to talk with Mr. Deimeister 'cause he's too busy getting some kid out of the basketball hoop who keeps yelling, "It was just a bet, it was just a bet."

I ate all my lunch today 'cause word got round that we didn't have the trampoline in gym class. I usually don't eat much on gym days. Not since that real bad tuna casserole day that my stomach just couldn't take. (Of course, there was also the unfortunate incident where I tripped over the lunch lady and landed in the sloppy joes . . . but let's not get into that.) Anyway, only saltines on gym day, that's my rule.

But what happened today was better than no trampoline.

It was better than no dodge ball or volleyball. It was better than no field trip to Ice-Skating World or the rock-climbing wall at the Wellness Center. The only thing better than none of these things was no Mr. Deimeister taking us to all those places.

Story is he had a nasty fishing accident over the weekend and he won't be back for a couple of weeks.

It's better than Halloween and summer vacation all rolled up in one. It's better than three desserts and no curfew. It's better than a water main break in school or a snow day that lasts a week.

What's really great is that there isn't a sub either. We all get to go to study groups. No sub gym teacher to carry on the trampoline evil.

Life is good—until I find out it's a lie in fifth period and I'm going to have to dress and head out onto the gym floor like every day before with a substitute teacher who will follow all the lesson plans that Mr. Deimeister left behind.

Vic, whose foot is still healing, limps out beside me.

"Sorry, Jinx, I know you were counting on study group."

"Yeah, I was. But I'll be all right. I've flown off the trampoline before. At least this teacher hasn't seen me do it before."

But then I began to hear something.

It started low as I got closer to the gym door. Then I heard it a little louder. I moved quicker than I ever had getting to gym class.

There was music coming out of the gym. There was music coming out of *my* gym class.

It was square dance music coming out of that gym class. And beside the boom box playing that music was a bright shiny new gym teacher who had never gotten her nose broken by me!

Everything was going to be different. That little accident with Vic didn't mean anything. I'd be the fifth-grade champ of the world. Just me—all by myself.

All I could do was smile as the substitute explained how we were to line up and which hands we had to grab of each other's to dance. I don't even remember her name, this wonderful teacher who brought square dancing to us.

She started the music up again and everybody started moving to the words she called out. All I remember is Josh running at me to swing me around . . .

In a few minutes I didn't remember anything for a while.

They say I have a concussion and a sprained ankle. Josh only got a big bruise on his forehead.

I had to stay in the hospital for two days. I've had a lot of visitors, though. Most of my gym class came the second day and brought square dance music for me.

The nurses weren't happy.

I even got a visit from Mr. Deimeister, who was on the third floor and wheeled himself down to visit me. He smiled when he rolled himself into my room and heard the music.

"I thought you had a concussion, kid," he said, looking at my bandaged foot.

I shrugged. "How do you get hurt *fishing*?"

He shrugged back. "I didn't know my reel would

14

snap. I must have broken it somehow and not known it. Anyway, I was reeling a big one in, and out of the boat I went. Just a few ribs and some cuts, a concussion and a collapsed lung. I'm okay."

Oh, no. A broken reel?

Naaah.

"So. How was it?"

"How was what?" I say.

"The square dancing. I called the substitute to suggest it. I take it you were the one who left the music in my office."

"Oh yeah, that was me."

"Well, it looks like you missed the square dancing. Sorry. I thought you'd be safe from the trampoline while I was gone."

"Mr. Deimeister, I didn't get here because of the trampoline."

The look on poor Mr. Deimeister's face made me laugh so hard, I almost fell out of the bed. The nurse came in and said she thought I'd had enough visitors, but I kept laughing because I knew then that I was never going to be a square dance champion.

So what else could I do but laugh?

Angela Johnson's School Report

Favorite Class: English

Least Favorite Class: Math

Best Teacher Ever: Wilma Mitchell, third grade

Worst Smell at School: Stewed tomatoes on bread

Favorite Cafeteria Meal: Pizza burgers, corn, potato chips, and chocolate milk

Best Prank Ever Played: Getting a teacher to look through our classroom door, and then singing, "How much is that doggy in the window?"

The best time in gym was when: we square danced! (Of course.)

Best Field Trip Ever Taken: To Spain or the petting zoo when my best friend got chased by a pig

Best Memory: The last day of school in sixth grade. Four of my friends and I had a picnic in the woods and sang stupid songs until we lost our voices.

Some of the books I've written are: *Toning the Sweep* (a Coretta Scott King Award winner), *Heaven* (also a Coretta Scott King Award winner), and several other novels and picture books for young readers. One of my most recent novels is *A Cool Moonlight,* published by Dial Books.

HOW I GOT MY ENGLISH A

by Avi

Peeple that spel well and have good gramar are mostly freeks.

I no that for sur.

Stop and think of all the peeple you no. How many good spelers are there??? Not so many!!! As for gramar, I have one at home—my mother's ma—who I do truly love. So why another gramar at school?

Do I make my point? You bet. Better even—I'll tell a story. It tells how me and my english teecher were kidnaped together. You might think that was the worst news ever, but it turned out to be the best thing. It changed my hole life.

I'll start where it began.

Wonct upon a time—as most storys start—there was this miss cannister or how ever she puts it. She was an english teecher. *My* english teecher.

We got on only so and so. She was always on me about my talking too much and speling too little. Also, lots of time when I got jumpy she wood send me to the suply closet in the basement so I could shake my legs and cool my mouth. Mostly, she was always telling me that my riting was no good. I would go, "Hey, I no what I'm talking about and my friends no too so how come you dont? Besides—what good do speling get anyone anyhow? I'm not going to be no dumb author. If I want some covers I'll get in bed, not in some book. Ha ha."

She wood smile—she did hav a nice one—but then she wood put down a mark for me which was usually toward the end of the alfabet (XYZ), not from the front side (ABC).

I wonct told her that if she gave me some more of those front end letters, I wood have a pocket full and could use them to spel a lot better. She laff with that joke.

But then she sez, "The way you spel tells me the kind of person you are."

"I can hardly spel the alfabet," I sez. "Whats that make me?"

"A boy who needs to stay in school."

Lots of times she sez if I would only reed I would be lots better.

I sez, "I do reed."

"What do you reed?" she sez.

"The funny papers."

She sez, "So thats why your so funny."

We laff and that was that.

In other ways she was tuff. You had to be nice in class and most of all never do no cussing. She sez, "Cussing was the devil's language." And she would have nuthing but proper english in her class.

Now since I was not much good in school and always fooling a round so as to make the class have some fun, miss cannister had me stay in after three lots of times. When I sez a lot, I mean bunches. When you make people laff you pay a price that aint funny.

Anyway, since I was there, and I was big for my twelve years—sometimes I would run errands or help her. Which is what happened that day.

It was right after book fare day—dont you worry, I never got one—which meant that the buy money was in the big safe in the school basement. The safe was next to the suply room that was full of paper and pen stuff.

Miss cannister sez, "Pokey"—which is what she would sometimes call me—"please go fetch me a box of paper from the suply room cause I need it for next week."

"Sure," I sez. It was already neer four clock because I had been reely no good that day. And I was restless and cheeky. "What exactly is the stuff you want?"

"Maybe I'll show you," she sez, "because its not jest any paper I want but some speshul kind. But its hevy and I can use you to bring it up." I'm nuthing if not strong.

So we go down the steps. It is dim down there with only one week light on a wire that hangs down like an upside down lollypop. But then there wasnt suppozt to be any one there but us since its so late and not many like me have to stay in. Also, I dont think many teechers like miss cannister work so much. I think that she works so hard because she cant find anyone smart as her to spend her fun time with. It would take a smart dude to marry up with her. Xtra smart.

Anyway we were down there in that room looking for her box of paper when a sudden noise comes.

"Whats that," she sez.

I sez, "I dont no."

"I think some one else is also heer," she sez.

"So what?" I sez. "Its a free country."

"Not that free," she sez. "No one is suppozt to be around but us."

"Well then less go see," I sez.

"No wait!" she sez, but shes too late because I go anyway and I guess she thinks—since she is the teecher—she should go with me. Which is not smart but she does it anyway.

So we go out there and gues what. There is this guy there which I never saw before. He was neeling at the safe. Which is okay—its not my money. But miss cannister screemed.

Quick as anything this guy jumped up and pointed this gun at us and sez, "Hands up!!!!"

Well, natch, we do.

"What are you doing here?" sez miss cannister, who can be, like I tol you, tuff. "This is school property," she tells the guy.

"I'm stealing from the safe," he sez. "Who are you?

"Shes the english teecher," I sez, "and I'm her best student," you no, just for laffs.

But he sez, "If you are so smart maybe you can open the safe."

"Not me," I sez.

"Not me neether," sez the teecher.

He looks at us cross. Because what he does—is cuss a purple puddle.

"Dont you dare talk that way," snaps miss cannister who is always ready to correct anyone since she is an english teecher. I mean, she would correct God if He didnt up and sez things with the rite english.

But this theef comes rite up to her and sez, "I'll talk the way I want." And just for spite, I gues, he swears again, but even worse. It was so bad both my ears tingled at the same time.

I could have tol that man it was a mistake since miss cannister was so tuff about bad words. If she sez it once, she sez it a million: "Take the high road and you will see further than with the low road."

Sure enough, she halled back and slapt him real hard—*crack!*—on the face. Trouble was, she slapt him so hard she hurt her han. I can see that because of the way she held that han in her other han.

The theef didnt notice. He just got angry.

"Get in that room!" he shouted. "I'll make you pay for that." With that gun of his he got us to go back to the suply room. When we do he sez, "Youll stay in there till I let you out. If I cant get to that safe I'll hold you for handsom."

"Whats handsom got to do with it?" I sez. "Your ugly."

"Shhh," sez miss cannister. "Show respect for your elders and do what he sez."

So we do and he shuts the door on us.

We sit there for a while and miss cannister is working her han where she slapt him. "It hurts," she sez. "I think maybe I broke it. It is my rite han to," she sez.

"I'm sorry," I sez which I truly was.

Well after a while the theef with the gun comes back and sez, "I cant open the safe. Rite a handsom note and I'll get money that way."

"My han is broke," sez miss cannister. "I cant rite."

"Well," he sez, "let your favorite student rite it."

"Who, me?" I pointed to myself.

"Yes, you."

"I dont rite too good," I sez.

"Dont give me that," he yells. "Rite it."

"Better try," sez miss cannister. "Theres plenty of paper and pencils here."

So I fetch some and with them two looking at me I look at the paper. "What do I rite?" I sez.

He sez, "Tell them I've got you both and I'll kill you unless I get one thousan dollars."

I sez, "You mean, nine hundred and ninety-eight for her and two cents for me?"

"Just rite it," he sez and points the gun as if he means it.

So I take up the paper and a pencil and I rite:

handsom note!!!!
Miss cannister and me are hold up
by a guy with a gun and he sez you
mus bring one thousan dollars to the
school, or else we are dead meat.
                    Poky

When I was done the theef grabbed the letter from

me and reeds it. "This is so badly ritten," he yells. "No one will believe it. If this is your best student I would hate to see the worse."

I wood have sez something smart, but there was his gun which was reel. I could reed that all right.

"Let me see it," sez miss cannister.

He shove it at her.

"Well, yes, it is poorly ritten," she sez and gave me a look which I no very well because it always means I'm going to get a letter from the back end of the alfabet again.

"You rite it," the theef sez to miss cannister.

"My han is broke," she sez.

He stands there for a moment and swore again, another not of nasty words. "This is the worst speling I ever red," he shouts.

"I suppose you are a good speler," sez miss cannister to the theef but she sez it like she don't meen it—all sarcastic.

"I spel very well, thank you," he sez.

"All right then spel chic-can-ary," or some such word.

He pops out with some letters.

"Thats good," she sez. "What about ren-o-grade."

He spels that one too. With the rite letters too, I gues. Because this goes on for quite a while, with miss cannister asking words and the crook putting up the letters with pretty good sense. A speling test, sort of. In fact, the more it goes on the more miss cannister is impressed.

In fact she finally sez, "Mister, who ever you are, why, if you spel so good, are you a crook? You should be ashamed of yourself. Good speling is hard to find. You could be an upstart citasun."

He looked pleased by that. "No one ever heard me spel before," he sez.

"You should be proud of yourself, not some crook. You have a reel skil," she sez.

And so what did that man do? Sure as simple, he started to cry!!!

Pretty soon miss cannister and that crook are talking up a quiet storm and dont care about me at all.

In fact they got to talking so much I got bored and took my handsom note and went home. And I was thinking that poor guy, if he didnt care for speling so much he would have been a thousan dollars richer. But no, not him!

Of course I didnt tell anyone what happened cause I figured it wasnt all done yet. I mean, good storys have a way of ending in their own direction. And not always a happy direction either. So what I did was rite down everything that happened just in case that guy came after me and murdered me for loosing his handsom money. I mean I wanted people to no my being killed was not my fault—just my speling.

But gues what? Two months later miss cannister and that crook got married!!!!

But before she did it she took me a side and told me, "*Please* do not say anything about the man and how I met him. He is reformed now."

See, being such a good speler she was helping him become a english teecher just like her.

"But I already rote all that down," I sez.

"You did?" she sez all surprised. Maybe it was because I had never ritten anything on my own before.

"I truly did."

"May I see it?"

"It probably has speling mistakes in it," I warned.

"I dont care."

"You dont?"

"Not this time."

So I gave her what I rote.

Only thing, she never gave my riting back to me. Instead she gave me an A back—the furst I ever got in english so I guess I did rite good after all.

In fact, it made me think that riting wasnt so hard. I just might become a riter after all.

Avi's
School Report

Favorite Class: History
Least Favorite Class: Spelling
Best Teacher Ever: Mr. Mal

Camera shy

Worst Smell at School: Kids throwing up in the closet

Favorite Cafeteria Meal: Didn't have a cafeteria

Meanest Thing: Being left out

Best Time in Gym: Didn't have a gym

Best Field Trip: Christmas visits to the bank

Some of the books I've written are: *The True Confessions of Charlotte Doyle* (which won a Newbery Honor Award), *Nothing But the Truth: A Documentary Novel* (a Newbery Honor Award winner), the best-selling Dimwood Forest series, *Crispin: Cross of Lead* (a 2003 Newbery Award winner), and over fifty other books for children.

EXPERTS, INCORPORATED

by Sarah Weeks

There are three things in this world I can't stand—cucumber salad, wool sweaters, and creative writing. Cucumbers make me burp and wool makes me itch, but if you gave me a choice, I would rather burp and itch at the same time than have to write something creative.

"You finished your essay, right, Rodd-o?" my friend Lucas asked me as we walked toward school together early one morning.

I hesitated. Lucas is my best friend and we always shoot straight with each other.

"Yeah, I finished it," I said.

"Phew, that's a relief," he said. "If you hadn't, I would have to kill you, you know."

"Yeah, I know," I said.

The problem began on the first day of the school

year when our humanities teacher, Mrs. Greenberg, promised that if nobody got an F in her class all semester she would give us a pizza party.

"Just remember," she'd laughed, "there are no F's in *pizza*."

Here it was, the last week of the semester and I was about to earn not just an F, but the F that would ruin everything. Because, you see, I hadn't done the assignment. Not one word of it.

As we rounded the corner and headed up the block toward school, Jeremy and Russell, two friends from our class, caught up with us.

"You guys did the assignment, right?" Russell asked us.

"Yep," Lucas answered for us both. "How about you?"

"Of course," said Jeremy. "What do we look like, idiots? I can taste that pepperoni already. Last year's class got the party and somebody told me she let them have all the soda they wanted too."

When I get nervous, I sometimes get hives on my neck, and I could feel one beginning to prickle up under my collar.

"What profession did you pick?" Lucas asked.

"Doctor," Jeremy said. "'Cause they get to save people and stuff."

"I picked truck driver," said Russell. "They get to travel and eat at diners. I love diners, but my mom says they're too greasy, so we never get to go. What about you, Lucas?"

"Star pitcher for the New York Yankees," he said. "Man, can you imagine getting paid to play baseball?"

The assignment had been to write an essay about what you want to be when you grow up. Sounds easy enough, unless you're like me and have no idea what you want to be, and no matter how hard you try, you can't think of even one thing that feels the least bit right.

"I bet all the girls are going to say they want to be teachers 'cause they know Mrs. Greenberg will eat that up with a spoon," Russell said with disgust.

"Yeah, probably," Lucas agreed. "So, what did you pick, Rodd-o?" he asked, turning to me.

We were just starting up the steps of the school, when a familiar cry went up from the playground.

"Hey look, everybody! There goes Mucus! Hey, Mucus!"

Lucas blushed and hung his head as we walked up the steps and into the building. It happens to him all the time, poor guy. He has one of the worst names. Not only does *Lucas* rhyme with *mucus,* but even if you shorten it to *Luke,* you're still in trouble because then it rhymes with *puke.* He's been tortured his whole life on account of that name.

Having a bad name is something Lucas and I have in common and probably part of the reason we became friends all the way back on the first day of kindergarten. My name is Rodney Curtain. My parents and my teachers call me Rod, my friends call me Rodd-o, and my sister, who's only two, calls me Rah-rah. Rodney Curtain may not be the greatest name in the world, but front-ward like that it's not so bad. The thing is, at school when they call out your name for attendance they say it backward. Lucas Bromberg becomes Bromberg, Lucas. Samantha Smith becomes Smith, Samantha.

Unfortunately, I become Curtain, Rod. That's bad.

As we made our way down the hall to home-room, I felt sorry for Lucas on account of the teasing, but secretly I was relieved that he'd forgotten about the question he'd asked me. How was he going to take it when he found out I hadn't done the assignment?

After she took attendance, Mrs. Greenberg—we have her for homeroom as well as humanities—announced that she would be collecting our papers after lunch. There was still hope left. All I had to do was come up with an idea between now and then, scribble it down in time to hand it in with the others, and maybe I wouldn't have to ruin the party after all. The problem was, I still didn't have any ideas.

"What do I want to be?" I asked myself. "Come on, Curtain, think."

I thought about it during math, history, and science lab, but with lunchtime only minutes away, my mind was still a complete blank. The only thing I could think of that I wanted to be was someone else. Someone who had written the stupid essay already.

As I looked around the room desperately hoping to find some inspiration somewhere, I asked myself,

"Do I want to be a scientist? Do I want to fix clocks? Write books? Build desks? Make pencils?" No, no, no. And then suddenly without warning, everything shifted into slow motion as my eyes came to rest on the face of the girl sitting in the second seat in the third row from the left. That's when it hit me. I knew what I wanted to be. What the world needed me to be.

When the bell for lunch rang, I didn't join the others in the cafeteria.

Instead I took out my notebook and began to write. When the fifth-period bell rang, I was already in my seat in Mrs. Greenberg's room with a stack of four handwritten sheets of paper in front of me and a huge grin on my face.

"Why are you sitting there smiling like a dork?" Lucas asked as he slid into the seat next to me. "And where were you at lunch anyway? And another thing, you never answered my question from before, what did you choose as your profession?"

"Name expert," I told him happily. "That's definitely what I want to be, a name expert."

"A name expert? Whoever heard of that?" he said.

"Nobody. It hasn't been invented yet. But I'm going to be the first one," I told him.

"Oh, yeah? And what exactly are you going to do?" he asked me.

"I'm going to advise people about what not to name their kids."

"No offense, but that is so dumb. Why would anybody pay you to tell them what not to name their kid?" he asked.

"Because I'm an expert," I said.

"Says who?" he said.

"What's your name?"

"What do you mean, what's my name? You know my name, fish-for-brains." Lucas snorted.

"Come on, just answer the question. What's your name?"

"Lucas," he said.

"And what do all the kids call you?"

He hesitated uncomfortably for a second before answering.

"Mucus," he said quietly.

"Exactly," I said. "See? If I had been around when your parents were deciding what to name you, I could have warned them that every name needs to be checked for bad rhymes. A kid named Leo is gonna end up getting called B.O., anybody named Gabby is gonna get called Flabby, it doesn't take a rocket scientist to figure that out. Your name is particularly bad, because it's a double whammy."

"Tell me about it," said Lucas, shaking his head sadly.

"The way I see it, a name expert should be hired every time a baby gets born, to protect it from being saddled with a name that could ruin its life," I went on.

"How much do you think you'll get paid?" he asked.

"A lot. Parents pay a bundle for braces to straighten their kids' teeth. Don't you think they'd shell out even more to save their kids from being humiliated at school?"

"Here's a question for you—do you think there's any way a name expert could figure out whether a name is going to fit when the kid gets older?" Lucas asked me.

"What do you mean?" I said.

"Well, for instance, you know how Melody Adams is tone-deaf?"

"Yeah, she sings like a moose," I said.

"If her parents had known she was going to be unmusical, maybe they wouldn't have given her a musical name like Melody."

"Maybe they would have named her Moose," I said. We both laughed.

"I suppose a name expert could be trained to look carefully at the parents for signs of what's to come," I said. "Like for instance, if there's a history of baldness in a family, it's probably not a very good idea to use the name Harry."

"Yeah, or like if the parents have big noses they shouldn't name their kid Honker," said Lucas.

"Who names their kid Honker?" I said. "That's not even a real name."

"Oh, and Curtain Rod is?"

I punched him in the arm, but not too hard because like I said, we're best friends.

"Hyphenated names would have to be looked at very carefully too, don't you think?" Lucas said. "Like Jessica's, for instance."

"Exactly," I said. "She's the one I was looking at in science lab when this whole idea came to me."

Jessica dad's name is Charlie Mintz and her mom's name is Sylvia Pepper.

How hard could it have been to name her Jessica Mintz-Pepper instead of Jessica Pepper-Mintz? If they'd had a name expert around, trust me, it never would have happened.

"You know, I take back what I said about this idea being dumb," Lucas said. "I think maybe you're onto something big here."

"Yeah? You think?" I said.

"Yeah. And you know, once business takes off, you might even need a partner," Lucas said excitedly. "We could call it Experts, Incorporated."

"We?" I laughed. "I thought you were going to pitch for the Yankees."

Lucas smiled and shrugged.

"I doubt I'll get picked up; I can't even throw a slider. But if you want a partner who really understands why the world needs name experts, I'm your man, Rodd-o."

Mrs. Greenberg came down the aisle collecting

the papers. As I handed her mine, I heaved a huge sigh of relief. Not only had I avoided ruining the pizza party, I'd managed to plan my entire future too, and it was looking pretty bright, if I do say so myself.

Sarah Weeks's School Report

Favorite Class: English and orchestra (I played the viola.)

Least Favorite Class: MATH, always MATH

Best Teacher Ever: Mrs. West, even though I hated her at the time

Worst Smell at School: Fish sticks in the lunchroom

Best Smell: Freshly mimeographed paper—it was before Xerox machines and the ink smelled sooooo good

Best Taste: Paste, which we were not allowed to eat, but of course, we all did

Favorite Cafeteria Meal: Butter sandwiches (My mom always used margarine at home, but the butter tasted so much better!)

Meanest Thing Someone Ever Did to Me: Made fun of my flowered underwear when I was turning flips on the rings on the playground. I went home and asked my mom to buy me all white underwear after that.

Gym was always the best: when we did tumbling, which is what we now call gymnastics. I was especially good at walking on my hands.

Best Field Trip Ever Taken: Apple picking—I was always the tallest in my class, so I could reach the best apples

Best Memory: Playing a Christmas ornament in a play in first grade

Some of the books I've written are: *Regular Guy, Guy Time, Guy Wire,* and most recently *My Guy* (which is being developed by Disney for a feature film). I've also written many picture books for younger children, including *Mrs. McNosh Hangs Up Her Wash* and *Follow the Moon.*

APPLE BLOSSOMS

by Terry Trueman

I've got to read a poem in front of the whole class. There's no way out of it. Actually, this shouldn't be that hard for me. I'm kind of the class clown, always messing around, teasing other kids, acting stupid, and saying funny things. Even my teacher, Ms. Souza, laughs with everybody else when I'm joking. She's cool. So how hard should it be to do an "oral interpretation" of a poem—I guess that just means to read it out loud? No biggie. The truth is, I like it when everybody looks at me and laughs at the stuff I'm joking about. It's fun. I like to make people laugh. So, oral interpretation? Big whoop—I'm always relaxed when it comes to being the center of attention.

This class clown thing is fun. I think to do it you have to have a certain kind of personality, which

I've got. Don't get me wrong, there are drawbacks. If I were *just* a class clown, I'd be seen as basically an idiot. Fortunately, I'm also good at sports, so I'm used to playing two different roles, the jock and the joker.

Here's what I'm saying: When teams are being picked on the playground, like for football or baseball, and all of us are standing around trying not to look nervous as the captains pick who's gonna be on their teams—right then, my being the funniest guy in class doesn't mean squat. The captains only care about getting the best players they can—period. It doesn't make any difference how good an imitation I can do of the principal, or how many jokes I know. Joking around can't help me catch a football, or hit a baseball, but I always wind up getting picked early, first or second. Like I said, I'm good at sports.

I'm even better, though, at the joking thing. It's not like anybody ever says, "Oh, there's Jason Truman, official class clown," or anything, but everybody knows I'm funny. Ms. Souza even uses me to get the other kids to do their work sometimes—like if everybody's bored or restless, Ms. Souza will tell them, "If you buckle down and do your work, I'll let Jason do a skit." That's what she always calls it, "a skit," like I'm a professional comedian. But the truth is, my skits are never planned out. I never know what I'm going to do in front of the class when I first go up there. And Ms. Souza never asks me if I want to do a skit or not—she just tells me to do it.

I don't know where I come up with my ideas, but once I'm up there, if everybody in class is laughing, I just keep doing whatever I'm doing. Like last week, I started making some stupid faces, then snarling, then making a cross-eyed, toothy-grinned, "dumb and dumber" type of expression, not getting tons of laughs, and then I got an idea: I pretended like I was a thousand-year-old man, all bent over and confused-looking—this old man was nasty and gnarly too, kinda pulling his pants up so high that he'd almost have to open his zipper to spit. And I had this old man scratchin' himself all over, especially his butt. I used Ms. Souza's big wooden yardstick as a cane to help my old man stumble around the room. I made it look like he didn't have any teeth, wrapping my lips so they looked like my gums and smackin' 'em back and forth while

I mumbled in this real old voice about "young whipper-snappers" and "back when I was yer age, there was this Tyrannosaurus Rex that lived down the street" and stuff like that. Everybody in class was laughing, so I knew I was doing my job.

Once in a while I say or do something that goes overboard, maybe gets a little *too* freaky, and Ms. Souza gives me "the look" and everybody tries not to laugh, and that's usually the end of my "skit"— but Ms. Souza always calls on me again, so she must not get *too* mad.

Back to this poem-reading thing, though. Having to read this poem in front of the whole class is a little bit different than being a jock or clowning around. First off, it has to be a serious poem. I mean, our assignment says that the poem is supposed to be about war. I haven't been able to find any funny poems about war. Most of the poems are pretty bloody and sad and all that; they're all about guys' friends getting killed and blown up and donkeys dying and brave heroes and all. A lot of the poems are old too, like a hundred years old and about World War I.

And they're really long too—I mean really long, like a whole page or even longer. Because they're poems, they don't make much sense either. I guess because these poet guys were trying to rhyme everything, maybe their teachers didn't care as much about them making any sense—especially since they were writing about their friends and innocent donkeys getting blown up. I don't know for sure.

I *do* know that after a long time of searching I've managed to find the shortest war poem I can find. It's about springtime and war. It's only eight lines long and real easy and I even sort of understand it—the guy thinks war is pretty bad. Something like that. Anyway, I'm good.

Because it's so short, I don't even have to practice reading it very much. I know all the words, so what's the point in wasting a lot of time just reading it over and over again?

I say it a couple times, not out loud, but to myself, and then I turn on the TV. Like I said, I got it. Springtime and war, eight lines long—spring is nice, war is bad. Big deal. It's gonna be easy. All night long the poem, which I've copied out on a sheet of notebook paper, lies on the table in front of me while I ignore it.

Every once in a while my mom hollers in, "Are you practicing your poem?"

And I yell back, "Yeah, sure, I'm all over it."

When nothing good is on TV, and I've channel surfed for as long as I can stand it, I play video games. I even play a war game for a while, so I figure I'm good to go.

Today's the day. Ms. Souza asks for "volunteers." I think the war poems have taught us that it's not a very good idea to "volunteer," because nobody raises their hand. Ms. Souza calls on Fred Gritten, whose desk is next to mine. I think to myself, Close call. It's like having a mortar shell land on the guy in the trench right near you.

Fred gets pretty nervous and scared in front of people. He's just that way. Fred's not very good at sports either. He's not terrible, like some guys, but he always gets picked toward the middle. I guess everybody figures that you're not gonna win or lose by having Fred Gritten on your team. I like Fred, though, because he always laughs harder than almost anybody else when I'm joking around, and he always tries hard at sports.

Earlier in class this morning, I kept looking over at Fred, and he was practicing his poem over and over again—moving his lips and staring at the page like it was a bomb that'd just landed in his lap.

I whispered, "Relax, Fred, you're gonna give yourself a heart attack."

He looked at me, and his eyes looked really scared. "I know," he whispered back. "I feel like that."

"Take it easy, man," I said again. "It's just reading a poem."

Fred said, "I know, but I don't want everybody to laugh at me."

That made me think. Every time I get up in front of the class, I'm *trying* to make people laugh. But now, with this oral interpretation about war and death and all that, I knew just what Fred meant— it'd be pretty bad if everybody laughed when you're trying to be serious.

Still, as Fred gets up to go read his poem, I whisper, "Charge!" kind of loud. A couple of kids sitting around us giggle.

Fred goes up there and his hands are shaking and his face looks white. I have no idea why Ms. Souza picked him to go first. She's like a general, sending some soldier to a certain death for the good of the regiment. Poor Fred.

Fred's poem is pretty long and has foreign words in it and makes no sense at all. It's about guys getting gassed and dropping dead with yellow faces, but Fred's idea of oral interpretation is just to read the poem, one word after another, as fast as he can, including the foreign words, until he gets to the end. He doesn't look up from the page at all, and when he's done, he lets out a big sigh and hurries back to his seat.

Nobody laughs at Fred, though, and I don't even tease him, because now we're all waiting to go up and take our turns. It's like waiting to get chosen for the front lines or picked for sports. I'm just sitting here until my name is called, until it's my turn to march up there. I'm okay, though. I keep reminding myself that my poem is short.

Ms. Souza calls on some other kids, Allen Mender, Graham "Cracker" O' Neal, Amber Quarentino. For some reason, sitting here waiting my turn, I start to think about being the class clown, about how I need to not clown around when it's my turn, but about how funny it would be if I acted like an idiot during my oral interpretation—like if I turned into that thousand-year-old man again, mumbling and stumbling all over the place, maybe crawling back home from the war with a hand grenade stuck up my . . .

I laugh and suddenly Ms. Souza is staring right at me. Amber has just finished and is walking back to her chair. She's giving me a killer look, like she thinks I'm laughing at her oral interpretation—which I'm not. I wasn't even listening.

Ms. Souza says, "So, are you ready, Jason?"

I look at her. "Sure," I say.

A couple of kids snicker, kids who laugh at *everything* I *ever* say, so I add, "Ready for duty." A few more kids laugh. Not Fred, though. He's sitting real quiet, like he's shell-shocked.

As I've been half-listening to the other kids, I've figured something out. "Oral interpretation" isn't just reading the poem as fast as you can like Fred did. Ms. Souza keeps telling everybody to "slow down" and think about "the meaning of the poem." I know for sure that some of my friends could go a hundred times as slow and I still wouldn't have a clue; especially not about the poems with part foreign words like *dolcey esty decoration is* or whatever.

I make my way to the front of the room. The same kids who laugh at everything I say, laugh at the way I'm walking, so I break into a gorilla walk, swinging my arms down and leaning way over from one side to the other, then back again. Even more kids laugh. Ms. Souza doesn't laugh, though, so I stop messing around and try to get serious as I stand in front of the class.

I want to get a good grade on this, but I'm feeling weird. My palms are sweaty, and there are little trickles of sweat under my arms. My hands aren't shaking, like Fred Gritten's were, but I feel tight in my throat, like I should cough or something. Suddenly I think to myself, I wish I'd practiced reading my poem out loud. Too late now, but I wish I had.

I put my sheet of paper onto the podium thing, and I put my hands on the side of it. My palms are so sweaty that I'm sure my hands will leave little wet spots, but I try not to think about that.

I look out at everybody. Their stares, their expressions, make me feel even more scared. Are they expecting me to joke around, even though they know I'll get killed if I do? I realize now that I don't really know what my poem is even about. I mean, I know the springtime and the war and that the first line is something about guys marching and stuff.

I'm feeling more and more nervous, looking out at everybody. A couple more kids, plus the first kids who laughed earlier, start to smile.

Ms. Souza asks, "Are you ready, Jason?"

More giggling from the troops.

"Sure," I say.

I think to myself, The heck with oral interpretation, I'm just gonna read this kind of slow and pretend I understand it and get it over with. It's only eight lines long.

I start to read the poem and I get through the first line. I have no idea what I've just said. It's like there's a battle raging all around me and inside me. My nerves are racing and exploding. I can't think straight. I start to read the second line and now I hear myself. It's about the soldiers in springtime and they're marching along and the poem says what they can smell . . .

"The scent of assel bloppems fills the air . . ."

I freeze.

What did I just say?

Did I just say *assel bloppems*?

What's an assel bloppem?

There's a soft, horrible gasp from the class. Now the room is deadly quiet. I keep staring at the page; eight short lines, it begins to swirl.

What did I say?

Where am I?

I find my way back to the start of the line and try again. "The scent of . . ." I hesitate for half a second, I can do this, I can say this . . . but it's so quiet, so tense . . .

"The scent of . . . assel bloppems . . ."

The roar of the class laughing drowns out the rest of my words.

"What?" I mumble. "What'd I say? What'd I say?"

Nobody answers, I'm not even sure they can hear me through all their laughter. In all the clowning I've ever done, all the times I've tried to make kids laugh, I've never heard laughter as loud or long or real as this before. But when I look up at Ms. Souza, she isn't smiling. Fred isn't laughing either; his expression is worried, like he wishes he could rescue me.

My face goes bright red; I can feel it. Now sweat is pouring down from my armpits like somebody turned on a faucet.

Without knowing I'm going to say it, I blurt out "Assel bloppems" again.

Everybody roars even louder. Their laughter becomes explosions, bombs going off, bullets and shrapnel flying all around my ears. Kids are doubled over, almost falling out of their chairs, they're laughing so hard. My head is dizzy. My vision blurs. I can't see the words of the poem anymore; I can barely even see the page.

Finally Ms. Souza says, "That's enough, Jason. You can sit down."

I think to myself, No, I'm not done yet, I have to read the other six lines.

But when I look at Ms. Souza, I can tell that I'm in trouble, that if I say another word, especially *assel* or *bloppems,* I'm a dead man.

I make my way back to my seat. No gorilla walk

this time. I hurry, trying to be invisible as I move. This doesn't work; I can see the joy, the wild excitement in most of the kids' eyes. But I glance at Fred and his look is one of sympathy for a fallen comrade. I think to myself, Assel bloppems, assel bloppems, apple blossoms . . . What did I say . . . apple blossoms . . . apple blossoms . . .

I turn to Ms. Souza and yell at the top of my voice, *"Apple blossoms!"* She jerks in her seat, as if I'd just yelled *"Incoming!"*

"That's enough, Jason," she says, an angry tone to her voice. Everybody stops laughing and the room is silent.

Fred whispers to me, "You got it, you can do it . . . good job!"

I'm standing right next to my seat by now, I cry out, my voice loud and clear. "No! I've got it, I can say it, really; I can. Listen . . ."

"Jason . . ." Ms. Souza tries to interrupt.

But I can't stop myself, I yell loud and strong, "The scent of assel bloppems fills the air . . ."

Whatever calm and quiet Ms. Souza's stern voice just commanded is lost in the roar of my classmates' laughter. It's like a battalion vaporized, like a whole army annihilated. Fred shakes his head sadly.

"Jason!" Ms. Souza snaps.

I can only think of one thing to do, there is only one thing left to say. I mutter, "I surrender."

Terry Trueman's School Report

Favorite Class: Recess, although I'm aware that technically it's not exactly a class per se; then again, neither is lunch, my runner-up

Least Favorite Class: Anything to do with numbers . . . m-a-t-h, for instance

Best Teacher Ever: Kay Keyes, twelfth-grade creative writing teacher and saint!

Worst Smell at School: Some things in the boys' locker room in baskets—socks, I think, but who knows?

Favorite Cafeteria Meal: Pizza

Meanest Thing Someone Ever Did to Me: I was the guy who handed out nicknames and I was merciless— I refuse to go into details, just in case there's no statute of limitations for such crimes.

Gym was always the best: when I wasn't there.

Best Field Trip Ever Taken: The only one I remember is going to the University of Washington campus, where I carried around a copy of *Webster's Collegiate Dictionary* because I thought it made me look like an intellectual.

Best Memory: I forget . . .

Some of the books I've written are: *Stuck in Neutral* (which won a Michael A. Printz Honor), and my most recent in the U.S. is called *Inside Out*. I also have a new novel in the United Kingdom called *Swallowing the Sun*. I'm currently hard at work on the next novel.

SCIENCE FRICTION

by David Lubar

Oxygen met hydrogen.

Phaboom!

Twenty-seven kids jumped out of their seats like they'd been jabbed with forks. Not me. I saw it coming. There was Ms. Adler, wearing safety goggles and a goofy grin, holding a pair of test tubes mouth to mouth. Any science geek would know what to expect. I spotted it before class, while everyone else in the room was chattering and fooling around. The tubes had been sitting in a small tank of water. A wire ran from a battery terminal into each tube. Break up water with electricity, you get hydrogen and oxygen. Slowly. Put the gases back together, you get water again. Quickly. And a bit of a bang. Energy has to go somewhere.

I loved Ms. Adler's class. I want to be just like her when I grow up.

"Do I have your attention?" she asked.

I understood the need for loud displays. It was our first day back from spring vacation. Everyone was probably still cranked on chocolate bunny ears and marshmallow eggs. As I said, energy has to go somewhere.

"It's project time," Ms. Adler said. "I'm going to divide you by random into groups of four. Speaking of which, who can define *random*?"

"I know," Benji Halbers shouted from his seat in the back row. "There were two squirrels in my driveway, but then my dad random over."

Most of the other girls in the class and a bunch of the boys went, "Eeew." Not me. Scientists need to remain calm and detached, even when faced with the thought of splattered squirrels.

Ms. Adler sighed, but she didn't quite manage to hide her smile as she scanned the raised hands. She called on Ellen Stover, who stood up, grinned, straightened her skirt, and said, "*Random* means you don't know what it will be."

"Sort of," Ms. Adler said. "But I think we can get

a bit more precise. Even if you don't know what a present will be before you unwrap it, that doesn't mean it's random."

"I got this for my birthday," Ellen said, holding out her left hand so we could all admire the extremely ugly ruby ring that clung to her pinky like a swollen zit. "It was a surprise."

Sheesh. It wasn't enough for her that she was pretty and smart and rich—she had to make sure everyone knew all the details of her life.

"Very nice, Ellen," Ms. Adler said. She called on several other kids, then finally pointed at me. "Amanda?"

"Each member of the group has the same chance of being selected," I said.

Ms. Adler nodded. "Exactly. So, with that in mind, write your name on a piece of paper."

I flipped through my notebook and hunted for a blank page. I found one in the back. Then I hunted for a pen. I finally found one inside my eyeglass case.

Ms. Adler collected our sheets in a box. "Now, I'm going to randomly pick groups of four."

Benji stood up, swung an imaginary golf club, and shouted, "Fore!"

Ellen asked, "Can't we pick our own groups?"

Personally, I wished we'd be put in groups of one. I do my best work on my own. But if I had to be in a group, I'd rather not leave the details to chance. Some of the kids just weren't serious about getting good grades.

"I'll tell you what," Ms. Adler said. "Let's make an exercise out of it. I understand you want to work with your friends. We're comfortable with familiar things. But comfort doesn't always lead to surprising discoveries. So, what are the odds, if you select randomly, that you'll get the group you want? The first student who gives me the right answer can pick his or her own group."

Excellent. I'm not just a science geek. I'm also a math geek. I eat problems like that for lunch. Well, that and turkey sandwiches on whole wheat bread. I glanced around the room to see how the competition was doing. Most of the kids were staring at their calculators as if the keys were marked in Martian. A couple were actually punching in numbers. Randomly, I hoped. And, off to one side, George Mastiff was staring at the wall. He was new, he was big, and he was silent. He kind of spooked me. I didn't think he'd talked in class even once since he'd arrived here last month.

"The odds keep coming out even!" Benji shouted.

I hunted down my calculator, which had somehow wandered from my backpack to my purse, solved the problem, and gave Ms. Adler the answer right before Ellen raised her hand.

Ms. Adler nodded. "It looks like you get to pick your group." She shuffled through the box and removed my name.

"Great." I looked around the room and realized I'd never actually worked with any of the others. But I saw a couple of kids I figured I could get along with. "I'll take—"

"Not so fast. I said you could *pick* your group." Ms. Adler shook the box. "Come on up and pick."

"Wait…" I wanted to argue. But all year long, Ms. Adler had hammered us over the head with one concept. Science requires precision and attention to the smallest detail. You couldn't be sloppy. You couldn't make assumptions. I'd just done that. And she'd gotten me.

But heck, I was a good sport. And I wanted to be a good scientist. So I went up and reached into the box. I figured I still had a decent shot at getting a group that'd be willing to work hard for a high grade. I pulled out the first sheet.

Oh, no. No, no, no, no, no.

Benji. The Joker himself. He was so hyper, he didn't get sent to the office anymore because even the principal refused to listen to him for more than ten seconds.

I started to jam the sheet back in the box. Ms. Adler cleared her throat. Loudly.

I handed her the paper, then pulled out the second name.

Noooooo . . .

Ellen. Ms. Perfect. The only girl in the school who had different colored pens to match each of her outfits.

And the third.

George. Of course, of course. A boy who had less to say than Benji's squirrels.

What were the odds of that? I felt like I'd won the lottery and then discovered that the prize wasn't a million dollars—it was a million dead fish.

I returned to my seat and listened numbly as Ms. Adler explained the details. "You can choose any scientific field you want. The project must represent the combined work of all members. It will be due in seven weeks and count as half your grade for the marking period. You'll have to work on this on your own time, but I'll give you a couple of minutes in class to get organized."

I stood up and looked around. Unlike oxygen and hydrogen, some things didn't combine very easily. For example argon, neon, and the other inert gases. Or the four of us. Ellen and George didn't move. Ellen obviously wanted everyone to come to her. George didn't seem to care who went where, so I walked over to his desk. So did Benji. Ellen had no choice except to join us.

"Hey," Benji said, spreading his arms wide, "group hug."

Ellen and I both went, "Ewww." Some things were too gross even for calm, detached scientists.

"Just kidding," Benji said.

"Knock it off," I said. "We need to get organized."

"Who said you were in charge?" Ellen asked.

"I'm good at science," I said.

"So am I," Ellen said. "And I'm organized." She held up her notebook, which was disgustingly neat.

My notebook looked like the wrapper of an exploded firecracker—which didn't mean I wasn't a good scientist. I'd just been too busy to straighten it out. Though I'm sure I could never get Ellen to believe that I knew what I was doing.

I tried to think of a scientific approach to picking a leader. Meanwhile, George reached into his pocket and pulled out a quarter. He flipped it onto the back of his left hand, covered it with his right hand, and looked at Ellen.

"That's no way to pick," she said.

He looked at me.

"Heads," I said.

Heads it was.

"So, when shall we meet?" I asked.

It turned out that they had stuff going on all week except for today right after school. Three coin tosses and a short argument later, we agreed to meet at my place.

"My room's a little messy," I warned everyone.

"Messy room, messy mind," Ellen said.

"Empty room, empty head," Benji said.

Much as I hated to admit it, I was starting to like him.

We met outside after school and walked to my house. On the way, Ellen mentioned thirty-seven reasons why she was so great and wonderful and perfect, Benji made nineteen jokes, and George kicked a rock.

When we went inside, my mom got all excited. "Oh, you brought friends, Amanda. How nice. I'll make snacks." She seemed to think I spent too much time by myself.

"Watch your step," I warned everyone as we approached my room. I pushed against the door. It didn't move. I leaned into it and gave a hard shove.

"Eeew. You want us to go in there?" Ellen scrunched up her face like she'd been invited to enter the wrong end of a sewer pipe.

"Hey—it's not dirty. It's just messy." I walked over various piles of clothes, books, magazines, and other essentials, then plopped down on my bed. Okay—actually, I plopped down on the clothes that were on my bed.

Ellen tiptoed in, followed by Benji and George. George sat on my hamper. Ellen perched on the edge of a chair. "You should fire your maid," she said. "Ours would never leave a room like this."

I ignored her.

"Wow. It's sort of like you live inside a laundry basket." Benji walked over to the highest mound of clothes, right near my bookcase, and reached up. "Hey, I can touch the ceiling." He thumped his chest and shouted, "I'm king of the crap pile!"

"Cut that out," I said. "We have work to do."

"Knock, knock." My mom appeared with a tray stacked full of goodies. Before anyone could speak, she'd handed each of us a plate. Turkey sandwiches, and baby carrots with little dishes of ranch dip. Mom made great sandwiches.

"Okay—back to the project," I said. "What about chemistry?"

"Boring," Benji said.

George nodded.

I took a bite of my sandwich. I really loved chemistry, but I was willing to compromise. "Biology?" I asked.

"Not interesting," Benji said.

George curled his lip.

I took another bite, and tried another field. After getting similar responses from them for everything I could think of, I looked over at Ellen, who'd been sitting quietly, eating her snack. Even there, she was disgustingly neat. I didn't see a crumb on her plate. She'd finished her sandwich and started on the carrot sticks.

"You like chemistry?" I asked her.

"Astronomy," she said, dabbing a speck of mayonnaise from the corner of her lip with her napkin.

That figured. I bet if I'd mentioned astronomy, she'd say she liked chemistry. We kept talking, but got absolutely nowhere. Ellen didn't like any of my ideas. I didn't like any of hers. Benji seemed more interested in touching the ceiling and waiting for someone to mention astronomy again so he could make gross jokes about the seventh planet from the sun.

And George just sat there. Though, compared to the noise everyone else was making, I had to admit I was beginning to appreciate the value of silence. We only had an hour because Ellen needed to leave for a piano lesson. When it was time to go, we agreed that everyone would think about stuff for a week. Then we'd get back together.

"Nice friends," my mom said after they'd left.

"Wouldn't you like to have a neat and tidy room where all of you could hang out?"

"It's fine the way it is," I said. I'd rather spend my time trying to understand the universe than straightening out one little unimportant part of it.

We met the next week. Mom brought snacks again. And once again, we couldn't agree on anything. Finally, I said, "Look, we can't keep going like this. If we don't pick a project now, we're toast."

"Planning is important," Ellen said.

"So is toast," Benji said.

"But we aren't planning, we're arguing," I said.

"We are not," Ellen said.

"We are too," I said.

"Are not."

"Are too."

"R2-D2!" Benji shouted.

"You're the only one who's arguing," Ellen said.

We argued about that until it was time for her to go.

Third week—third meeting. We might as well have been in third grade. Ellen and I argued. Benji seemed fascinated by his ability to touch the ceiling near my bookcase. I actually thought about moving that pile of clothes, but I sort of hated to spoil his fun. George kept his thoughts to himself, though he did seem interested in checking out some of the books I'd stacked up next to the hamper, which surprised me.

We finally agreed that since we couldn't agree on a project, everyone would bring an idea next week and we'd vote for the best one.

Week four. I voted for my project. Ellen voted for hers. Benji voted for Albert Einstein. George didn't vote, but he did offer the use of his quarter.

"Look," I said. "It's obvious we can't agree. So let's each start an actual project. Next week, we'll pick the best one, and everyone will work on it."

Week five. We each decided we needed another week. Everyone left right after our snack. When Mom came back for the dishes, she sniffed, looked at my piles of clothes, and said, "You really need to think about picking up."

She was right. It was getting a little stuffy. But I couldn't pick things up just then. I needed to think about my project. So I found a more elegant solution. I opened a window.

Week six.

"What's that supposed to be?" I asked Benji when he lugged his project into my room.

He looked down at the pile of Popsicle sticks and coat-hanger wires attached to a board with bits of duct tape, bent nails, and large globs of glue. "It's a roller coaster."

"You're kidding."

He shrugged. "It sort of fell apart. I'm not great with tools."

I figured he'd make a joke about the project, but he just sighed and said, "Sorry I let the group down."

I looked over at Ellen, who hadn't brought anything. "Did you start a project?" I'd expected her to drag in a display charting the life cycle of Gucci handbags.

"I tried to spot comets," she said. "It would be so great to discover a new one. Dad bought me this excellent telescope last month. But it's been cloudy every night."

I waited for her to say she was sorry, but she didn't. I guess the word wasn't in her vocabulary. I glanced at George. He shook his head and spread his empty hands. Then I looked at my desk, where I'd balanced a large board that contained my experiments. I'd grown crystals in various solutions. "I guess we'll have to use mine," I said. "Notice how the copper sulfate produces a—"

Just then, Mom appeared in the hallway with a tray. She pushed at the door. Then she pushed harder. There still wasn't enough space for her to get in. She gave the door a good, hard shove. I could feel the floor shake.

On my desk, the whole display started to slide. I tried to dash across the room, but I tripped on a pair of jeans. All of my hard work crashed to the floor.

I lay on my stomach, staring at the icky mess. Mom put the tray down in the hall and squeezed through the doorway. "That's it. I've had it. This room is a disgrace." She grabbed a handful of clothes from the floor. I expected her to drop them somewhere, or toss them. Instead, her eyes opened wide. Then she went, "Eeewww."

I looked over. Under the clothes was ... something. It was dark green and shriveled. *What in the world is that?* I leaned closer. "Oh, my God!" It was some kind of food.

"That does it!" Mom yelled. "You are grounded until this room is clean."

"But—"

"Disgusting." She shook her head and walked out.

I stood there, staring at the *thing*. Whatever it was, I hadn't put it there. I was a slob, but I wasn't a pig.

Behind me, Ellen whispered something.

I spun toward her. "If you mention your maid one more time, I'm going to scream."

Ellen flinched and backed away from me. I realized I was already screaming.

"I just wanted to tell you I was sorry," she said.

"What?"

"I'm sorry. It's my fault."

"Your fault?"

She shrugged. "I'm allergic to wheat."

I let her words roll around in my brain for a

second, hoping I'd somehow misunderstood what she meant. But the equations only seemed to have one solution. Ellen didn't eat bread. Ellen's plate was always empty. Ellen had just apologized. "Are you telling me you've been stashing sandwiches in my room?"

"Not sandwiches. Just the bread. The turkey was delicious."

"Why?"

"I didn't want your mom to think I didn't like her food. And I felt kind of funny about mentioning my allergy. I try so hard to fit in, but it's not easy sometimes. I'm not good at it like you are. You're just so comfortable with stuff."

"What?"

"You don't worry about what people think," she said. "I worry so much that I always end up saying the wrong thing. And you're so smart. I have to study so hard. I have to keep everything so carefully organized, or I get lost. But you—you're so good at science."

"Oh." I'd definitely need to think about what she'd just said. I guess I'd been making a lot of assumptions. But at the moment, I had a more urgent issue to deal with. I looked at the moldy slab. "How many?"

"Every week," she said.

"Where?"

She went to various clothes heaps in my room and revealed the slices of bread, which ranged from slightly moldy to totally overgrown.

Benji picked up the pieces and laid them out on my desk. If the bread hadn't been buried in my wardrobe like some sort of ancient Egyptian funeral offering, I probably would have found it pretty fascinating.

"I'm sorry," Ellen said again. "I'll explain to your mom that this was my fault. And I'll help you clean your room. Okay? If there's one thing I'm really good at, it's straightening up." She looked at me like she expected me to turn her down.

She seemed really sorry. "Sure. You can help. That would be wonderful."

"I'll help too," Benji said.

George nodded.

"Thanks," I said as we tackled the top layer. "This is great. But we still don't have a project."

"Sure we do."

I was so shocked by the voice, I just stared at George.

"We do?" Benji asked.

George nodded and pointed at the bread.

"Mold!" Ellen said. "We have a whole display of the stages of mold growth."

"Yeah," I said. George was right. We had pieces of bread for each week. "But is that enough?" It was hard to imagine a whole project from some slices of moldy bread. Then I realized it wasn't just about mold growth.

"Look," I said, flipping a piece over.

Ellen nodded. "Mayonnaise. It's acidic."

"Yup. We have an example of mold inhibition too. We just have to figure out a way to display it so you can see both sides."

"Great," Ellen said. "But what if it's still not enough?"

"Oh, there might be some more . . ." Benji said.

"What do you mean?" I asked.

"Promise you won't kill me?"

"No."

"Promise you won't make it slow and painful?"

"No."

He shrugged. "I sorta don't like turkey a whole lot."

"Oh, please don't tell me you've been stashing meat in my room."

He nodded.

"Where?" I sniffed and looked around.

Benji pointed at the top of my bookcase.

"You slimeball," I said as I climbed a chair to take a look. Oh, yuck. There were five piles of turkey in various stages of decomposition, neatly laid out from left to right. It was absolutely disgusting. It was also pretty fascinating. And I guess I was relieved to know the smell wasn't coming from my clothes.

I looked over at George. "What about you? Is there anything you don't like?"

He lifted a stack of books to reveal baby carrots.

"Good grief. How could all of you just hide food away like that?"

"Well," Ellen said, "the place is kind of a dump. If you don't care, why should we?"

"When in Slobovia," Benji said, "do as the Slobs do."

I couldn't argue with them. All they'd done was

sink to my level. Maybe this was one area where it wouldn't hurt for me to try to be a bit more like Ellen. But just a bit. No way would my pens ever match my wardrobe.

We got back to work. At five, I asked Ellen, "Don't you have a piano lesson?"

"It won't hurt me to miss one." She flipped open her cell phone and made a call.

Right after that, George left. I figured he had some sort of appointment he couldn't cancel. But I was grateful he'd helped for as long as he could.

There was still plenty to do. The rest of us kept working.

"I found it!" Benji screamed a couple minutes later.

"What?" I asked.

"The floor!"

I stared down at the spot where he pointed. "So that's what it looks like."

"Nice rug," Ellen said.

"Thanks. I forgot I had one."

Just as we were finishing, George returned, holding a beautiful display case with sections for the bread, turkey, and carrots. It even had mirrors in it to show both sides of the specimens.

"Wow," I said, "that's perfect. Did you build it?"

He nodded.

"You're a genius with your hands," I said.

He smiled.

Ellen patted him on the shoulder. "And you don't waste time talking unless you have something to say."

"I'll do the captions," Benji said. He started coming up with these awful puns that made everyone groan, like, "Spore score and seven weeks ago," "Rot and roll," and "Bacterial Girl." But we laughed too. And I knew Ms. Adler had a great sense of humor, so I figured it wouldn't hurt to use Benji's titles.

Ellen, who had beautiful handwriting, lettered the signs. I typed a report to go along with the display. As we all finished up the project together, I realized I'd discovered an important scientific principle. It had nothing to do with mold, but everything to do with chemistry. Some elements combined quickly. Others combined slowly. And some didn't combine at all unless you mixed them together under high heat and intense pressure.

We got an A. Ms. Adler complimented us on our planning. "I'm impressed," she wrote, "that you worked so nicely as a group and immediately got started on a well-planned and complex project. Your use of familiar food items was especially clever."

That afternoon, as I was leaving school, I found Ellen, Benji, and George waiting for me.

"Want to hang out?" Ellen asked.

"Do you?" I asked back.

All three of them nodded. I thought about those reluctant elements again—the ones that didn't want to combine. When you finally got them together, they usually formed incredibly strong bonds.

"Seems a shame not to take advantage of all our work cleaning your room," Ellen said.

"Good point." I didn't have the heart to tell them that half the floor had vanished again. They'd find out for themselves soon enough. On the other hand, it would give us something to do. There was one other thing I had to tell them, though. "This time, I think we should make our own snacks."

They all agreed about that too.

David Lubar's School Report

Favorite Class: Art

Least Favorite Class: Gym

Best Teacher Ever: Mr. Frendak, a very cool science teacher

Worst Smell at School: Me after gym

Favorite Cafeteria Meal: Open-face roast beef sandwich with brown gravy (at twenty-five cents a sandwich, this is one of the many reasons I was so bad at gym)

Meanest Thing Someone Ever Did to Me: I think I blanked out all the worst stuff.

Best Prank Ever Played: Passed around a note that said, "Look at the footprints on the ceiling." This is fun because each person stares up, realizes the note is silly, laughs, and passes it on. I got the idea from listening to the great humorist Jean Shepherd.

The best time in gym was when: I made a basket all the way across the gymnasium during a kickball game in fourth grade. Sadly, it was also the high point of my entire school athletic experience.

Best Field Trip Ever Taken: Bronx Zoo

Best Memory: Getting an unexpected invitation to

Ellen Lebowitz's party. Thank you, Ellen, wherever you are.

Things I've written: I've contributed to several short-story collections. My novels include *Wizards of the Game, Flip, Dunk,* and *Hidden Talents,* an ALA Best Book for Young Adults.

The grade? School Zone

Written by James Proimos · Illustrated by david fremont

Panel 1: Every day of my life is exactly the same. I'm talking exactly.

That's right, you are about to enter a world of sights and sounds that you must keep repeating. You are about to enter **The Grade School Zone!**

Panel 2: Every morning my grandma sits in her chair and waits for the school bus.

Panel 3: I'm upstairs getting ready.

NY

Gentle Ben

waaaa! I can't find my other sock!

Panel 4: Every day just when I find my underwear I hear her yell.

Yipes!

The Bussa!

85

She says "Bussa" instead of Bus because she's from Italy.
Grandma came from here.
Italy
MAP
She messes up other words every once in a while. It's Fun.
I can no find-a my head. Where's-a my head
(She means "hat," not "head.")
Anyway, I always go running downstairs no matter what state I'm in.
Make Way!
But when I get outside I realize it's not my bus at all. It's the middle school kids' bus.
Hey Jim!
Grant middle
Hey.
So, I go back upstairs and just when I'm getting my pants on she yells again.
The BUSSA!

This time it's the high school kids' bus.
You don't have a shirt on, kid!
Coolguy High
BUS
I know.
snif!
So I go back in and then finish getting ready and then she yells again.
3
The BUSSA!
Are you sure?!
Yes-A!
You sure it's not the private school bus?!
It's-a goin' away! Hurrrry!!
By the time I get down it's too late.
Why you no listen?
Yep, that was my bus alright...
Hello
VROOOM
My mom has to drive me to school.
I would-a cry when there was-a no school.
Oh Grandma

The Second part of my day is spent explaining to my teacher that I'm not trying to be a wiseguy.
I have real questions but Mrs. Quinkle thinks I'm just trying to be difficult...
But how do we know we're made up of 98% water?
We do.
But what if I just had a glass and you hadn't drank anything in days?
bip!
Stop being a Weisenheimer, Mr. Proimos.
Why isn't my theory on how the universe began just as valid as George Lemaitre's?
Because he was a genius.
ho boy.
I could be one.
Probably not.
Why?
How can I teach if you keep asking silly questions?
If the Indians were here first, how could someone discover it?!
If you keep this up you are going to be sent to the principal's office!
But I...
ug.
GO!

Even my time with Principal Barbo is the same every day.
If you wouldn't ask questions to annoy your teacher, you would not be here every day!
I'm not trying to annoy anyone!
Yes you are.
No I'm not.
Yes you are.
No I'm not.
You are.
Am not.
Are.
Ain't.
Yes you are.
Yes I am.
No you're not.
I am.
I said you're not and that is final!
Hee hee

James Proimos's School Report

Favorite Class: Art
Least Favorite Class: Math
Best Teacher Ever: Ms. LeCore
Worst Smell at School: At my school it was the canned stuff the janitor sprinkled on fresh puke
Favorite Cafeteria Meal: I grew up in a half-Jewish, half-Italian neighborhood, so naturally the pizza bagels were top notch.
Meanest Thing Someone Ever Did to Me: Invent math
Best Prank Ever Played: I'm not a fan of pranks. Hate them.
The best time in gym was when: we filled everyone's gym shorts with shaving cream and . . . Just kidding, I hate pranks.
Best Field Trip Ever Taken: The trip to the chocolate factory
Best Memory: The only thing I have memorized from school are my multiplication tables. No matter how hard I try, I can't get them out of my mind.

Some of the books I've written and illustrated are: *The Many Adventures of Johnny Mutton; Johnny Mutton, He's So Him!; If I Were in Charge the Rules Would Be Different!; Cowboy Boy;* and several other picture books for young readers.

David Fremont's School Report

Nickname: Monk (because I was a good tree climber)

Favorite Class: Creative writing and art

Least Favorite Class: Math

Best Teacher Ever: Mr. Ficken

Worst Smell at School: Cafeteria

Favorite Cafeteria Food: Clown salad

Meanest Thing Someone Ever Did to Me: A girl used to chase me after school every day, corner me, and threaten to beat me up.

Best Prank Ever Played: Tying two aluminum cans to a fishing line and laying it in the street. When cars ran over it, they would hear a loud clanking noise.

The best time in gym was when: my head was slammed into a bench and I came to the realization that I had to start lifting weights.

Best Field Trip Ever Taken: The Hershey's chocolate factory because of the big blow-up candy bar

Best Memory: Coming in second place in the Pinewood Derby. Everyone laughed at my car, but I nearly won.

What I Do Now: Mostly I do animation, and I'm currently drawing a bunch of things that I hope will make it to television. This is my first illustrated piece for a book for kids.

THE DESK

by Lee Wardlaw

The first thing we noticed that morning was the smell.

One point three seconds after my best friend Tabby and I hustled into our sixth-grade class, she screeched in her tracks, wrinkled her nose, and demanded: "Eeew, Craig—what *is* that?"

"I don't know. . . ." I plunked my book bag onto a chair and sniff-sniffed.

Huh. It wasn't a *bad* smell. Not like the Dumpster at 3:30 on a blistering day when the cafeteria had served UFO (Unidentified Floating Objects) Stew for lunch.

Not like the juicy carcasses of my brother's socks after one of his high school triple-overtime basketball games.

No, it was a musky smell. An out-of-place smell.

An I-know-I've-smelled-this-before-but-can't-remember-*where* smell.

"Reminds me of a petting zoo," Tab said.

"The Three Stooges' water probably needs to be changed." I peered into the humid aquarium where Larry, Moe, and Curly, our White Australian Tree Frogs, glistened in their tropical home away from home. They ogled me as if to say: *Keep your big unwebbed hand out of our pond, you knucklehead!*

"Don't worry, fellas," I soothed. "Your water is just the way you like it—murky, not stagnant, with a twist of moss."

"Nyuk, nyuk, nyuk," Moe croaked.

"Craig!" Tab's voice scaled an urgent octave. "Look at The Desk!"

I didn't need to ask *which* desk. There was only one we'd wondered about, whispered about, all last week.

I whirled. The Desk sat shoved, as always, in the last row, far left corner. But someone had criss-crossed it with a spider web of hornet yellow police tape that read: CRIME SCENE. DO NOT CROSS.

We crept toward The Desk without a word, without a breath, as if afraid it might explode.

The door behind us opened with a splintering *crack!*

Tab and I levitated.

"Good morning, Craig, Tabby," our teacher, Ms. Chaltas, greeted us as she bustled into the room. Books and papers teetered in her arms. "You two are here early. Finishing your Greek project, yes? How's it going?"

"Ms. Chaltas—look!" Tab pointed at The Desk.

Our teacher glanced over, then shook her head and chuckled. "I knew there was more to that young man than he let on. Seems he had the makings of a practical joker. I'm sorry he isn't with us anymore."

My stomach bungee jumped to my toes and back. "You mean"—I gulped— "he's *dead*?"

"That would explain the smell," Tabby murmured. She squatted to squint at The Desk, examining it inch by inch as if expecting to find telltale evidence of murder: bloody fingerprints, a heavy crowbar, maybe a dangling body part.

"Dead? Of course not!" Ms. Chaltas plucked a pink slip of paper from within her book tower. "Just found this transfer form in my teacher's box. He's left the school. He must've expected it. He told us, his first day, he wouldn't be here long, remember?"

One week ago. Monday morning, early June. Silent Reading Time. All you could hear was the whisper of turning pages and the clock above the blackboard as it tick-ticked closer to lunch period.

The door opened without warning. Twenty-four heads swiveled toward the interruption.

My head stayed put. I was only seven pages away from finishing the most exciting book I'd ever read, and Did. Not. Want. To. Stop.

Tab nudged me, her charm bracelet clinking. I continued to read with my left eye while looking up with my right. That zinged me with a screwdriver-in-the-middle-of-my-forehead pain, so I saved my spot with a bookmark and focused on the door.

A boy had entered. Not tall, not short, but New. Ordinary too—except for the lime green grasshopper tattooed on his left arm.

The boy shuffled toward Ms. Chaltas, the tips of his ears as pink as the sheet of paper he handed her.

"People! Listen up," Ms. Chaltas announced with excitement. "We have a new student joining our class. A little late in the year, but better late than never. I'd like to introduce..." She paused to recheck the paper. "Ooo, this is a tongue-twister. Help me out here..."

The boy's pinkish ears bloomed deep rose. "I'll be gone before you learn to pronounce it," he said with an apologetic smile. "Just call me A and W."

"Like the root beer?" Tab asked.

"Just like." He waited as if expecting us to ask something else. When no one did, the smile vanished, making me wonder if I'd really seen it, if I'd only imagined he expected more.

"You may take Stacy's seat," Ms. Chaltas said. "Her family's already left on their summer vacation. Last aisle, back row."

Ears still pink, A&W shuffled kitty-corner from me to what would become The Desk.

The class resumed reading. A&W slid into his chair.

I dove back into my more-exciting-than-a-rollercoaster book.

Then, out of the corner of my eye, I noticed something strange.

A&W hunched forward, head low. He glanced right, left, right, like a spy on a secret mission assuring himself his actions were going unobserved. Satisfied, he tugged a flyer from his jeans pocket, scribbled something on the back of it, and folded it into a tight triangle.

When he noticed me watching, he put a finger to his lips, winked, and slipped the paper inside The Desk in a swift, furtive movement. He spent the rest of the period sitting straight, alert, guarding The Desk like a solider at his post.

"A and W is a weird nickname," I said to Tab at lunch while munching a tuna-and-green-olive sandwich.

"Weird to you, maybe," she replied. "I mean, people think Tab is a weird nickname for a girl until they learn the Why."

Tabby's last name is Stevens. Her parents were fans of the old TV program *Bewitched,* and named their daughters Tabitha, Samantha, and Endora after three witches on the show.

"You're lucky," Tab reminded me for about the 477th time that year. "Craig is a *normal* name. No one ever makes fun of it. No one ever asks you to wiggle your nose and do magic because of it."

"I wonder why he chose A and W, though," I said,

watching him from across the playground. He sat by himself (unless you count a sack lunch as company) by the tetherball court. "Does he have a bubbly personality? Does he love root beer? Is he the sole heir to the A and W fortune? Is there an A and W fortune?"

"We could ask him," Tabby pointed out.

"Yeah, I guess we could . . ."

But the bell rang, and we didn't. We were too busy doing end-of-the-year stuff, like building a model of the Acropolis out of Popsicle sticks, studying for tests, going to soccer practice, learning songs for the school Spring Sing, and, in our spare time, eating lots and lots of Popsicles.

Tuesday. A&W's second day at school. He slid into his seat just as the echoes of the final morning bell faded. He had dark circles under his eyes like the ones Tabby gets after one of Marlene Sikora's slumber parties.

"Please take out your math books," Ms. Chaltas instructed, "and do the problems on pages 173 and 174."

All of us banged, flung, or flipped open our desks and yanked out our books.

Not A&W. Like the day before, he hunched forward, head low. Then he glanced elaborately, secretly, right-left-right. Satisfied, he cracked The Desk and, holding his breath, slipped a slow, cautious hand inside, as if reaching into a basket of spitting cobras.

I nudged Tabby. We watched together as A&W eased out his math book. When he noticed us staring, he pressed a finger to his lips and winked. Then he closed the lid with a quick click and a deep sigh, as if relieved the cobras hadn't escaped.

"Pssst—hey," I whispered, noticing a flash of lime green on his right arm. "Wasn't that grasshopper tattoo on your *left* arm yesterday?"

He gave the apologetic smile. "Was it?" he answered, and opened his math book to page 173.

After math, the tattoo disappeared from A&W's right arm and reappeared beneath his right ear.

After science, it bridged his nose.

During Silent Reading Time, A&W wore it pirate-style, over his right eye.

"What's with the roving tattoo?" I wondered to

Tabby at lunch, while biting into a peanut-butter-slathered banana.

She shook her head. "It's like he's playing musical chairs with it or something. Look where it is now!"

I gazed over at A&W's usual place by the tetherball court. I could've spotted that blazing green a mile away. Especially since the tattoo was plastered smack dab in the middle of his forehead.

I laughed. "What's next—a tattoo on his *teeth*?"

"It's obviously a rub-on tattoo," Tab said. "He must have an endless supply of them. That's what he's guarding in The Desk!"

"Maybe his dad owns a company that *makes* rub-on tattoos," I suggested, "and this is a publicity stunt."

"We could ask him," Tabby pointed out.

"Yeah, I guess we could . . ."

But the bell rang, and we didn't. We were still too busy building our model of the Acropolis out of Popsicle sticks, writing speeches for the last-day-of-school promotion ceremony, losing soccer games, and, in our spare time, eating lots and lots of Popsicles.

▣▢▣

On Wednesday, the grasshopper tattoo had leaped out of sight.

Instead, A & W had the sniffles.

"Please take out your world history books," Ms. Chaltas said, "and turn to page 348."

A & W gave an apologetic sneeze. Then he began his now-familiar routine, the one he performed at least thirty times a day whenever he needed something from The Desk.

I nudged Tabby again to watch.

First, the hunch forward, head low.

Next, the secretive glances, right-left-right.

Then the painfully slow cracking of the lid . . . the easing out of the history book . . . the finger to the lips, the wink, the quick *click*.

And finally, the I've-kept-the-spitting-cobras-at-bay sigh.

A & W sneezed again. He recracked The Desk and eased out

—Tab and I held our breaths—

a silky, lime green handkerchief . . .

knotted to a sailor blue handkerchief . . .

knotted to a handkerchief the color of pizza sauce.

And still more handkerchiefs appeared, all tied

together, end to end: baby duck yellow, grape jelly purple, puce, lavender, olive, strawberry ice cream pink. A & W pulled and pulled until about a mile of the gauzy rainbow squares covered his feet.

He blew his nose—a short snort—into the last handkerchief (a piano key black), then reeled in the rest and eased them back into The Desk.

No one said a word. No one else had noticed. Tabby and I had been the sole audience to the show, and to the nine nose-blowing encores A & W gave at The Desk throughout the day . . .

"Please get out your math books," Ms. Chaltas began class on Thursday, "and take the quiz on page 231. Eyes on your own paper."

Bang, flung, flip.

Desks flew open. Math books were dug out. Pages riffled.

Tab nudged me with her tinkling, charm-braceleted arm, but I was already turned toward The Desk, watching, waiting, wondering . . .

What would A & W do today?

He hunched. He glanced. He cracked.

Out slipped his math book, a pencil, an apple.

And then—

A & W started to *juggle*.

Book, pencil, apple, book, pencil, apple. Around and around they flew, arcing above A & W's head as if he was doing something as easy as combing his hair, as easily as if gravity had never been invented.

Then—*thud, snik, cluf*—book, pencil, apple landed safely in his hands.

Tabby and I whirled to see if anyone else had noticed. Ms. Chaltas had her back turned as she wrote assignments on the board. Everyone around us sat poring over the quiz, pencils scribbling.

"Pssst—hey," I whispered to A & W, as he opened his math book to page 231. "Where'd you learn to do that?"

"Do what?" he asked with his apologetic smile, and nipped into the apple.

Friday. No tattoos, sniffles, handkerchiefs, or juggling.

They were replaced with a talkative stomach.

All through math, world history, and science, A & W's stomach gurgled and grumbled and groaned.

Finally, after recess, he hunched forward to open The Desk.

Tabby craned into the aisle to see.

A crumpled lunch sack appeared from the depths. With a minimal of rustling, A&W opened it and eased out a plastic container. He popped the lid and pinched out a cricket, a caterpillar, and an iridescent house fly.

Tabby's eyebrows disappeared up into the scrunchie of her ponytail.

I gulped. A&W seasoned his "snack" with a mini saltshaker. Then: one, two, three—gulp, gulp, gulp—he swallowed the bugs without a gag, without a blink!

"Did you see what I saw?" Tabby demanded at lunch, half fascinated, half grossed out.

"He ate *bugs*!" I replied, eyeing the coconut cookies my mom had packed, deciding they looked too much like hairy albino worms to eat. "Were they real bugs? I *think* they were real bugs. Maybe they were just gummi candies or something."

Tab shook her head. "I swear I saw the cricket's antennae twitch."

"But why would he eat bugs?" I wondered. "Is he trying to get attention? Is his family so poor, bugs are their only source of protein?" At the thought, I lobbed my entire lunch into the nearest trash can. "Or was it a trick? Maybe he's a magician! That's gotta be it, Tab. Think of the handkerchiefs, the juggling, the vanishing tattoos. The Desk has gotta be like a magician's trunk!"

Tabby tossed her lunch too. "Craig, that was too realistic to be a trick. I mean, those bugs looked exactly like the ones we feed the Three Stooges!"

"Oh, man," I said. "What if he ate *their* food? Or worse—what if Larry, Moe, and Curly are next on the menu?"

"We should ask him, I guess," Tabby said. "We've *got* to ask him!"

But we didn't. We were still too busy gluing together the final columns on our Popsicle Acropolis, cramming for more tests, burning CDs for Lucky Fitzpatrick's graduation party, and, in our spare time, bribing Samantha and Endora to eat lots and lots of Popsicles.

Besides, we figured we'd have plenty of time to ask him on Monday . . .

But of course, Monday arrived and A&W didn't.

"Craig, Tab, would you mind checking on Larry, Moe, and Curly?" Ms. Chaltas asked. "I smell something . . . *strange*. Their water might be brackish."

The bell rang. Ms. Chaltas scribbled spelling words on the chalkboard while the rest of our classmates swarmed in, buzzing around us as they took their seats, humming over the crime scene tape that ensnared The Desk.

"Ms. Chaltas," Tabby announced, "the aquarium needs to be cleaned."

"No, it—" I began before she jabbed me with a sharp elbow.

"Craig and I could scrub it during lunch," she offered.

"That would be wonderful," Ms. Chaltas said. "I have a staff meeting, but I'll leave the door unlocked for you."

Tab and I gave each other a Look.

Hers said: *Ha! We'll be here all alone! We can snoop in The Desk and finally find out what's in it besides bugs!*

Mine meant: *Oh, man! What if what's in there is worse than bugs? What if it's spitting cobras after all?*

At lunch, Tab karate-chopped the crime scene tape to shreds, her hand a machete hacking through a thick jungle. "Whew! What is that smell?" she asked.

Cobra food, maybe? What did cobras eat, anyway? Maybe I could spend the rest of lunch period researching that in the library...

Tab flexed her fingers above The Desk and said: "Ready? One, two—"

"No! Stop!" I cried. "I can't let you open it. There might be something dangerous in there."

She heaved a sigh. "Like a man-eating handkerchief, perhaps? A killer cricket?"

"I'm serious!"

"Then *you* open it."

"Are you *crazy*? There might be something dangerous in there!"

"Well, we won't *know* unless we *open* it, will we? C'mon, lunch'll be over in thirty minutes and we still have to clean the aquarium."

Still, I hesitated. "Maybe we should do that first.

If Ms. Chaltas comes back early and finds we haven't done it—"

"You're not *afraid* of The Desk, are you?" Tab challenged.

"Huh. I'm simply concerned for our safety."

"Nyuk, nyuk, nyuk," taunted Larry, Moe, and Curly.

Tabby rolled her eyes. "Well, *I'm* not." She grasped the desk to fling it open, but the lid wouldn't budge. "It's stuck. There's a ton more tape under here," she said. "Grab me a pair of scissors out of Denny's desk."

"How do you know Denny has scissors?"

"Denny 'Sticky Fingers' Porter? Of *course* he has scissors!"

I glanced over my shoulder, then threw open Denny's desk. "Whoa!"

"Find the scissors?"

"Only about six pairs! Plus five chalkboard erasers, four staplers, three rulers—"

"And a partridge in a pear tree!" Tabby sang.

"HEY! JUSTWHATD'YATHINKYOU'RE-DOIN'INMYDESK?"

Denny Porter stood in the doorway, fists on his

hips, scowl on his face. He flexed his biceps, making the muscles jerk like marionettes.

"Uh . . ." Tab licked her lips, thinking fast. "Um, we're conducting a survey. Yeah, a survey for Ms. Chaltas."

Denny thumped toward us, eyes narrowed with suspicion. "What kinda survey?"

"A scientific survey to determine what types of objects students keep in their desks," Tabby replied, her voice cool, calm. "It's required, annually, by the Board of Education, you know. Directive B.S. 117."

"Sounds fishy to me," Denny said, squinting harder. "You'll be growin' gills in a second. Hey, whatd'ya find in the New Kid's desk? Let's see . . ."

Tab protected The Desk with her body. "Sorry. Only authorized personnel allowed."

"C'mon, Tabitha," he wheedled in a fake, sweet voice.

"No."

"Maybe we *should* let him open it," I muttered, thinking of cobras.

"I betcha there's no such thing as B.S. whatever,"

Denny said, muscles twitching in a frenetic dance. He menaced closer.

"Take one more step," I threatened, "and I swear we'll tell Ms. Chaltas about you snitching the scissors and the erasers and—and the *you-know-what*."

Denny and his muscles froze. "Gotta go!" he said, and thundered out the door.

"The *you-know-what*?" Tab asked.

I shrugged. "Made that up. I figured if he was stealing school supplies, there had to be something even worse in there we didn't see."

"Brilliant, Sherlock!"

It was my turn to ask: "Directive B.S. 117?"

"Bogus Search, of course," she replied with a grin. She snatched a pair of scissors from Denny's desk and snipped the remaining crime scene tape. "C'mon, we're out of time. It's now or never. We've got to—"

"—open it," I finished for her. I took a deep breath and closed my eyes. "Okay, together on three. One . . . two . . ."

We lifted the lid.

"What the—?"

"What is it? What is it?" I scrinched open one eye.

The Desk was filled with straw. Stale popcorn. A wand of old petrified cotton candy.

"Ah, *man*!" Tab wailed, letting the lid shut with a disappointed slam. "Ms. Chaltas was right. A and W *was* a practical joker. This was a trick. A hoax. He's laughing at us all the way to his next school, him and his fake bugs and his vanishing tattoos, and . . ."

"Tabby—what's this?" Wedged between a hinge was a triangle of paper peeping out. It must've been the flyer A&W had slipped into The Desk a week ago, on his first day in class.

I nudged it loose with two fingers. Tab peered over my shoulder as I unfolded it. On one side it read in bold, curlicue letters:

THE WAJTKIEWICZ FAMILY CIRCUS
One Week Only!
Featuring Chills, Thrills, and Spills
Under the Big Top!
The Wondrous Wajtkiewicz Wire Walkers!
Pollyanna and her Prancing Ponies!
Sojourner the Sword-Swallower!
Marvolo the Magician!

Safari Sam and his Wild Cats!
The Illustrated Man!
and
The Bodacious Bug-Eating Boy!

With trembling fingers, I turned the flyer over. On the other side, A&W had scrawled in pencil:

It's a crime I never got to know you.

Sincerely,
Alexander Aaron Wajtkiewicz
(pronounced voit-KEV-itch)
A&W

Lee Wardlaw's School Report

Nickname in Elementary School: Lee-Pee

Favorite Subject: The Three R's: Reading, 'Riting, and Recess!

Least Favorite Subject: Math. The first book I ever published for kids was called *Me + Math = Headache*!

Best Teacher Ever: Mr. Cook. He took our sixth-grade class camping, let us decorate the classroom bulletin boards any way we wanted, and played Bill Cosby comedy records while we did seat work.

Favorite Cafeteria Meal: My elementary school didn't have a cafeteria, so every day, for five years, I brought a sack lunch from home containing a bologna-and-mustard sandwich on white bread, an apple, a bag of barbecue potato chips, and a Hostess cupcake. (I can't stand bologna now!)

Worst Smell at School: It's a toss-up between my desk (which was a rat's nest of old clay, dried-up Magic Markers, bologna sandwiches I never ate, and math tests with F's on them) and the garbage cans on the playground oozing sour milk at the end of a hot day.

Meanest Thing Someone Ever Did to Me: In fourth grade, I liked a boy name John Thomas. Not just liked liked. *Liked* liked. He found out, and to torture me he spent one entire recess chasing my best friend around the playground. Back in those days, if a boy chased and teased a girl, that meant he liked her, so I was very jealous and very hurt.

Best Prank Ever Played: Me? Play a prank? No, sorry. I was a *nice* girl. Then I grew up and wrote a book called *101 Ways to Bug Your Teacher*.

The best time in gym was when: "Best time in gym." Isn't that an oxymoron?

Best Field Trip Ever Taken: To the McConnell's ice cream factory. And yes, we got free samples!

Most Embarrassing Thing That Ever Happened to Me in School: I'm too embarrassed to tell you!

Best Memory: Singing with the girls in my rock 'n' roll group, The Shooting Stars, at the end-of-the-year school festival in sixth grade.

Some of the books I've written are: *We All Scream for Ice Cream!: The Scoop on America's Favorite Dessert; Bubblemania: The Chewy History of Bubble Gum; Seventh-Grade Weirdo; 101 Ways to Bug Your Parents; 101 Ways to Bug Your Teacher* and many picture books for young children.

THE CRUSH

by Rachel Vail

Walking down to lunch, she was next to me.
Gabriela Gonzales. She comes up to my armpit. I
have known her since second grade and always
noticed her, but never talked to her, never before
today, anyway. She has a really sweet smile.

As we were walking along, past the boiler room,
and then past the gym, I was thinking, This is the
time to say something to her. Right now. I had a
good thing to say too. I was thinking I could say,
"Gabriela, I really liked your dust mite feces report
today."

Some people kept going *eeew* and stuff like that
while Gabriela was giving her presentation, but I
thought it was really interesting. I will never look at
dust the same way again. Dust won't be just little
puffs of fluff to me now. It will be little puffs of

fluff with a lot of tiny bug poops in it. That is how good her presentation was this morning.

I wanted to tell her all that. I couldn't. No words came out.

Gabriela is tiny, but she was walking very quickly, chatting with her friends as they skittered toward the cafeteria.

I sat down at the other end of the table. People got quiet as I unzipped my lunch box. I am famous for my lunches. I make them myself, because it's like an interest of mine, a hobby, and besides, my mom used to rush it. Just slap some meat on bread, can of soda thrown crushingly on top. It's not her fault. She has enough to do and she's one of those people who don't care that much about food. I make Mom's lunch sometimes too, whenever she wants (otherwise she just has a yogurt and a banana, for her whole meal) and the people in her office are always impressed with what she takes those days. At least that's what my mom says, but she's like that. Complimentary.

She calls me a sandwich specialist.

Gabriela, on the other hand, takes the same thing every day: two slices of turkey on white bread, no crusts, probably mayonnaise. Hard to tell, with all that white. And she has either cut-up carrots or cut-up red peppers in a plastic bag, an apple juice box, and one vanilla wafer cookie. For me, her whole lunch would be an appetizer.

I pulled my sandwich from the bag. Some of the guys were getting impatient. Dave Calderon started to tear my tinfoil. I held up my hand. He calmed down.

I unwrapped the tinfoil myself. "Ooh," one of the girls from the other end said. I am pretty sure, unfortunately, that it was not Gabriela. She has sort of a squeaky voice, and this one was deeper.

"Pumpernickel," I explained. Mike Shimizo nodded. He makes his own lunch too, takes it as seriously as I do, and he's my best friend, but he is a sort of runty guy, real small, so he just can't eat all that much. But he does like interesting food, you gotta give him that.

I held up the sandwich so everybody could see.

"Tell us," Dave said.

I told them: mesquite wood smoked turkey, aged sharp Adirondack cheddar (one piece), de-seeded cucumbers, sliced grape tomatoes, one roasted red pepper, marinated in olive oil and capers overnight, cracked black pepper, and Dijon mustard.

Some kids said, "Mmm." Gabriela's best friend, Lulu, said, "Wow." Mike nodded again. "Unbelievable," he said. "The pepper."

"Yeah," I said. "I've been working with the balance. Last week I overdid it on the capers."

"No," said Mike. "The cracked black pepper. That's exactly right. It needs that, for bite. I wouldn't have thought of the cracked black pepper."

Mike looked sadly down at his spread. He'd done an old favorite—poached salmon on seven grain with tomato—which was delicious, of course, but he had brought it last Monday too. We both nodded.

I opened my club soda and took a big swig, then started to eat. The balance on the marinade was definitely much better than last week's.

I finished before Mike, but waited for him before we went out to the lower playground. It's basically a parking lot without cars, and a few basketball hoops without nets, but it's perfect for us. We don't need swings and slides and all that anymore—just a good open stretch of concrete with a fence around it, below window level so the teachers inside won't spy on us the whole time. The ones on lunch duty mostly stay up top, with the younger kids.

By the time we got out there, Dave Calderon and Lulu Peters were already captains, choosing up sides for Salugi, this game I think we invented back in fourth grade. Basically you have to get to your goal without being thrown down, and then you have to get through the goal, which are these little spaces under the fence out there. The small kids are really good for that part, because the bigger kids, like me and Dave and Evangeline Murphy, would never fit through those holes—though we are kind of good at grabbing the smaller kids' feet and not letting them through. Salugi has been officially banned ever since Evangeline gave Mike a bloody nose at it last year, but we play anyway. It's a really fun game, and a little collision with concrete never hurt anyone. Much.

Well, at least not until today.

Lulu picked me, so Dave got Mike. Mike is a great guy and really smart at school, up there in the top group with Gabriela in every subject. I'm in all the same classes as them except for math. I didn't do so well at it last year. My mom says it's okay not to be in the top group in math, but she's like that. I wish I were in that math class. But Mike, anyway, is a really nice person, as well as being very smart, but he even admits himself he will never go pro in Salugi.

We lined up in the center and started. It was a hot day, so I was sweating pretty soon. I love Salugi. The game was going really well, lots of interceptions, well-balanced teams. Evangeline is really strong, so she forced a couple of fumbles in the first few minutes, but Lulu made a great catch and faked out Evangeline beautifully, then tossed the ball to me. I caught it and started toward the goal. Lulu sprinted ahead and I saw her up there, wide to the right of the goal, just waiting to get the last-second pass. I knew we were going to score. I could already see exactly how I'd block Dave away from Lulu's feet.

I had maybe three of their defenders hanging on me, but I am strong, and I'd just eaten that really great sandwich—I could still taste the clean of the cucumbers blending with the smokiness of the turkey—so I was well-energized. I focused on Lulu's feet—just get to those tiny white sandals with the yellow and purple flowers, and we'll be up one–zip. That's what I was saying to myself when I tried to kick it up a notch, and, dipping my right shoulder to try to lose one of those defenders, plowed smack into Gabriela Gonzales.

What she was doing in midfield I have no idea. She is very small, one of the smallest of the small kids, so she should've been back by the other goal, in case somebody somehow got the ball away from me, but I have to say that the truth is Gabriela is even worse at Salugi than Mike. She kind of stands around until the action comes near her and then does this sort of skittering thing with her tiny steps to get away.

This time I guess she didn't quite make it.

I hit her full force with my shoulder on her back.

Still, I am not saying it is her fault or anything. I should've seen her there, near the sideline. I read somewhere that great ballplayers can see the entire field at all times. But I didn't see her at all until I'd already slammed into her.

She went up for a while before she came down.

It was sort of slow, how she moved through the air, more like a balloon (non-helium) than like a ball, when you smack it and it goes fast but then almost puts on the brakes, sort of takes its time going up, up, up, and then down, down, down. Like it's in no rush at all to get back to the ground, and why should it be?

Gabriela, once she eventually did get back to the ground, looked sort of startled to find herself there, a few feet from where she'd been standing just a few seconds earlier.

We all crowded around. I still had the ball tucked into the crook of my arm. "You okay?" people were asking.

"Gabriela?"

"Oh, no!"

"Eeew!"

"Look at her knee!"

We all looked at her knees, including Gabriela. One of them was fine. The other was not. It was split open. It wasn't bleeding much, but there was gook in it. It was a little horrible to see, honestly.

Gabriela's face went from surprised and pink to incredibly white. She made a little sound in the back of her throat.

I dropped the ball and without really thinking it

through, picked her up. I didn't want her to faint right there on the lower playground.

"Time out," I mumbled as I carried her toward school.

She rested her very white face against my shoulder and closed her eyes. I know this is very bad and selfish of me, when I should've been feeling more sympathetic about her bashed-up leg, but her head on my sweaty T-shirt felt nice.

"Sorry," I whispered. First thing I ever said to her: sorry.

She didn't answer. You can't blame her, I thought. It's gotta be hard to work up any politeness toward the guy who just crushed you, even if it was an accident and he's sorry.

I didn't say anything else, just carried her to the nurse's office. The nurse wasn't there. Some fourth grader lying on a cot with an ice pack on his ear said the nurse had gone to the teachers' room and would be right back. I wasn't sure what to do with Gabriela, where to put her—the fourth-grade sore-ear kid had closed his eyes, so he was definitely in no hurry to give up his cot-spot. I wasn't sure if Gabriela would want to be put on one of the plastic chairs or not. She still had her head on my sweaty T-shirt, so I just stood there holding her.

She is very tiny, but my arms were starting to fall asleep. I had to shift around.

Gabriela's eyes opened and she stared right into my face. She seemed surprised to find me there.

"Um," I said. "I liked your . . . bugs that poop in dust. Thing."

"What?"

"Project. Report," I said. "Science. Today."

A drop of my sweat fell onto her nose. I tried to wipe it away quickly, but I almost dropped her on the floor, moving my arm like that. She sort of yelped. I caught her. She wiped the sweat ball away herself and asked, "Dust mite feces?"

I nodded slightly. I didn't want to shake any more sweat balls loose.

"It didn't gross you out?" Gabriela asked.

"No," I whispered.

She stared at me for a few seconds, then smiled and said, "Thanks."

I forgot I should say "You're welcome," until she closed her eyes and lowered her head onto my shoulder again, and by then it was too late.

The nurse came back after another minute or so. She took one look at Gabriela's knee and said, "Uh-oh." I could feel Gabriela breathing faster, so when the nurse told me, "You can put her down and go back to class," I said, "That's okay."

The nurse called Gabriela's mom, sent the ear boy back to class, and told me to lay Gabriela down on the cot. I shook my head. "I ate a big lunch," I said, trying to explain why I wouldn't run out of strength. The nurse looked really confused, but I saw a small smile on Gabriela's mouth. She has such a sweet smile. She wasn't too heavy at all. I could've stood there in the nurse's office holding Gabriela Gonzales until the end of time.

Rachel Vail's School Report

Nickname: Didn't really have one, much to my disappointment (*Rachey* just doesn't do it.)

Favorite Class: Social studies and English

Least Favorite Class: Band

Best Teacher Ever: Mrs. Sudak, Mrs. T, Mrs. Barr, Dr. Murphy

Worst Smell at School: The locker of the girl next to mine in gym in high school

Favorite Cafeteria Meal: Peanut-butter-and-M&M's sandwich, not squished

Meanest Thing Someone Ever Did to Me: I am trying to get over all the mean things by writing novels about them. Beyond that, I will say nothing...

Best Prank Ever Played: Hmmm. I think I forgot to ever play a prank. I played the saxophone. That was pretty funny.

The best time in gym was when: Mrs. Powell said we should put our seats in the air and we had no idea she meant a part of our bodies.

Best Field Trip Ever Taken: We had an overnight trip in sixth grade to Washington, DC. I was going to sit with Karin, but then David called me and . . . Hmmm, that gives me an idea I might have to use in the book I'm writing now . . .

Best Memory: There are too many! Falling asleep in carpool. Friends coming over. Going to a friend's house. First day of school. Buying school supplies. The smell of my desk. New shoes. Terrifying tests. Discovering new books, new thoughts, new stories, new friends . . . There are so many memories, I have been spending my whole adulthood remembering, changing, combining what happened with what might have happened, what happened to somebody else, what I worried would happen, and what I hoped would happen into stories that happen to somebody fictional.

Some of the books I've written are: *Wonder, Do-Over, Ever After, Daring to Be Abigail,* the Friendship Ring series, a bunch of picture books, and, most recently, *Never Mind,* which I wrote with my good friend Avi.

THE GIRLS' ROOM

by Susan Shreve

The reason I'm in the girls' room with my feet up on the toilet seat so no one can see that I'm in this cubicle with the door locked is because I hate school.

I have been here since Special Reading second period with Ms. Burke. That's a long time and only one girl has come in and peed and washed her hands and left.

Already we've had third period and fourth period and now it's time for lunch. But I won't be having lunch today. I'll probably die of hunger, but I don't mind. It would be worse to be sitting at a long table and opening my lunch box, which is right now in my locker with a peanut butter sandwich and carrot sticks and a chocolate chip cookie my mother made last night. Ms. Burke might be on duty and look around the lunchroom with her pigeon eyes.

"Has anyone seen Zale Graver?" she'd ask.

That's my name. There are no other girls in the world called Zale, because my mother made it up.

"Zale's here," someone would say before I'd have a chance to slip under the table.

"Zale Graver. Come to my classroom immediately," Ms. Burke would say. "You can't have lunch or recess or gym until you read chapter one of your chapter book to me without mistakes."

That's what I'm afraid she might do, so I'm not going to move from this place in the third cubicle from the door, the only cubicle that has a lock.

So you're probably wondering what happened.

I can't read. I mean, I can read some things, baby books and even bigger books with some hard words and I can sound the words out very slowly. But so far, and I'm in the fourth grade, I have never read a whole book by myself. That's why I'm in Ms. Burke's Special Reading class. I also go to tutoring after school two days a week and in the summers.

⧉⧉

This morning I came into school a little late because I skinned my knee running down the front steps of my house, so I had to get a bandage. In my backpack, I had my copy of *Peony Bluefish and the Bag Lady,* which is my reading book for today. On the cover, there's a picture of this girl my age called Peony Bluefish, which I think is a stupid name for a girl. She is sitting in a rocking chair beside a very old woman who is the Bag Lady. The Bag Lady is wearing a dress that looks like a blanket, and there's a yellow canary on her head and a great big bag full of junk on her lap, which is why she's called the Bag Lady.

I was supposed to read the first chapter of this book for Special Reading class and I didn't have time. My mother said I did have time when I told her this morning I hadn't quite finished my homework.

"You could have read after dinner when you were watching television or before you went to sleep or even after school when you were talking to Esmerelda on the telephone," she said to me.

"No I couldn't," I said.

My mother is a single mom—that's what she

calls herself. My father lives in Daytona Beach with his new children, twin boys I've never met but I have seen their picture and they're not much to look at. Boys get spoiled, my mom says, so a girl has to be able to take care of herself in this world. And that is why I've got to learn to read pronto. *Pronto* is my mother's favorite word.

"Now, Zale," my mother said just the other night when she'd climbed into bed next to me to help with my reading. "I named you a special name because I knew even when you were a baby you would turn out to be a special girl deserving of such a name. So you can't let me down, sweetheart."

I don't want to let her down but I don't want to go to school either because it's too hard and the teachers, especially Ms. Carolina Burke, the jerk, don't like me as far as I can tell.

"School is too hard," I told my mother, but she just shook her head with this sorrowful expression on her face and said to me what I had heard from her many times before.

"Anything worth doing is hard, Zale. Hard until you learn to do it, and then it gets easy."

I didn't read *Peony Bluefish and the Bag Lady* because it was too hard. I tried. I really tried. I sat down on the couch when I came home from school and opened the book and read the beginning of chapter one.

"Peony Bluefish was an extraordinary girl who lived with her aunt Potato and uncle Fargo at the top of a clock tower in Butte, Alabama."

I'm sure you know now why I couldn't read this book. I didn't even understand the first sentence. I couldn't read the girl's name or extraordinary or Potato or Butte, Alabama. So I put the book back in my book bag, called my friend Esmerelda, which I do every afternoon, and then turned on the television until my mother got home from work at the supermarket. Every day when I hear her car pull up in front of our little house on Cedar Street, I turn off the television, take out my books, and pretend I've been working.

This morning when I got to school, I was too late for homeroom. I'd missed the roll and announcements and the special performance of the four top students in my grade reading their poems in honor of poetry month. I wrote a poem for poetry month myself, but I wasn't chosen to read it.

Starved for Poetry by Zale Graver 4x
 Give me a poem
 With two slices of rye bread
 Slap on some ketchup
 Make it mayonnaise instead.
 Cut the sandwich down the middle
 And pour me some Coke
 I'll eat the poem line by line
 And that's no joke.

Even my mother thought I should have gotten an honorable mention especially since she helped me with the spelling and made up the title.

Lela Bundle was just reading her poem to the class when I arrived and the homeroom teacher sent me straight to Ms. Burke's Special Reading, which was in the library. I walked very slowly to the library, stopping to talk to a first grader at the water fountain, waving to Esmerelda, who was in the other homeroom, arriving at Special Reading four minutes late. I checked the clock. Everyone was sitting around a long table with *Peony Bluefish* etc. opened to chapter one. Ms. Burke was asking questions about the chapter.

"Hello, Zale," she said when I sat down and opened my book. "Have you read the chapter?"

"Yes," I lied.

"Then maybe you could describe Peony Bluefish to the class."

"She's a girl," I said. I was beginning to feel like throwing up. I feel like that a lot in school.

"Yes. And what else do we know about her?"

I lowered my head and looked at the first page of chapter one, which was a blur before my eyes.

"She's friends with the Bag Lady."

"Yes, but we don't know that in the first chapter. The Bag Lady doesn't come into the book until the second chapter."

"So?" I was stalling for time, crossing my fingers in the hope that Ms. Burke would call on someone else.

"Tell me about her parents, Zale."

I took a guess. A "long shot," my mother would call it.

"They died," I said.

"They didn't die, Zale." Ms. Burke turned to Lisa True. "Do you know what happened to Peony's parents, Lisa?" Her voice was butter.

"They're on a trip in India and will be gone a long time, which is why Peony is staying with her aunt Potato," Lisa said.

Ms. Burke shook her head at me in that way she has as if she tries to like me but I am a constant disappointment to her.

"I don't believe you read this book very carefully, Zale," she said, pointing to Betsy Ford, who had her hand in the air. Betsy Ford always raises her hand, shaking it at Ms. Burke as if she has emergency information. I used to like her when we were in first grade, but she got smarter and I must have gotten more stupid, and now whenever I see her, I want to scream. Out, out, damn spot. That's what my mother says when she's in a bad mood instead of saying a swear word.

But before Betsy Ford had a chance to say anything, I raised my hand.

"I have to go to the girls' room," I said.

"No, Zale, you can wait," Ms. Burke replied.

I wiggled in my seat indicating that I actually couldn't wait, but Betsy Ford was talking about India and how her parents had gone to India on a business trip. That's the sort of thing Betsy will do. She raises her hand to answer a question and then she changes the subject, and by that time Ms. Burke forgets what the question was.

"I can't wait," I interrupted.

"Let Betsy finish what she is saying."

"I'm going to have an accident," I said.

Ms. Burke shot me one of those "you'll do what I say" looks, but already I had gotten up from my chair and walked across the library, pulled open the heavy doors, and headed down the corridor to the girls' room.

The girls' room at City Elementary is like every girls' room in every public school, only this one is painted turquoise and it has ten stalls. Ten stalls is a lot of stalls, but City Elementary has to have them because we're the biggest elementary school in the city. Two of the doors are off the stalls, one is hanging by the top, and all the locks are broken except the cubicle where I am hiding. But I told you that already.

There are six sinks, a long mirror over the sinks, a little shelf under the mirror, and about a hundred paper towels on the floor even though it's only eleven o'clock in the morning. No one bothers to throw the paper towels in the trash can.

So I figure I've been sitting on this toilet seat with my legs up for about an hour and a half. My stomach is growling and I wish I'd at least slipped the chocolate chip cookie into my pocket. I've read all the graffiti and there's plenty just in this stall. Most of the time, someone signs her name or draws a picture, and there are a couple of what Ms. Burke would call "dirty" pictures, which I won't describe, but usually the dirty pictures are of boys. There's an excellent picture in permanent black marker of a dog with long ears and a fluffy tail. *Boris was Here,* it says. And there's a big heart the size of my hand with *Mary B. and Tommy C. FOREVER.* And someone took the time to write a poem, so she must have been here for as long a time as I have. *Here I am/ Happy as a clam/ Sitting on a seat/Looking at my feet.* I mean, it rhymes. But that's about it for things to read in this cubicle.

I've been in trouble at school since first grade when the teachers found out I wasn't learning to read. At first, they were very nice about it. Ms. Foster would let me sit on her lap and she'd put her finger under the word and help me sound it out. And Ms. Roll, my second-grade teacher, helped me with reading during recess and gave me a cookie if I did a good job. Usually, it was a peanut butter cookie, which is my favorite kind.

But that was the end of nice. By the time I was in the third grade, the teachers thought I was doing badly because I didn't try.

"I work very hard," I told Ms. Burns, who was my third-grade teacher.

"If you worked very hard, we would see some results, Zale," she said to me.

My mother even called Ms. Burns on the telephone to say that she worked every night after dinner helping me learn to read and she knew I was trying.

It wasn't exactly true. My mother tried to help

me with reading, but it was easy to make her forget why we were sitting on my bed with a book open to chapter one. I'd start by telling her what had happened that day with Esmerelda or my other good friend, Train. I'd ask which mothers of my friends she'd seen come through the checkout at the supermarket that day. I'd tell her about a fight on the playground or about some of the older boys smoking behind the shed or trouble in the lunchroom. My mother was easily entertained by conversation and soon it would be nine o'clock, time for me to turn out my light, and very little work would have been accomplished.

By third grade, some of the kids in the class thought I was stupid.

"You're not stupid, Zale," my mother said. "You're smart. You just have trouble reading."

"No one else has trouble," I said.

"I bet you're wrong," my mother said. "I bet a lot of the kids in your class have a problem in reading or math or science or sports or singing. It's the way things are."

"Not at City Elementary," I said. "Everyone can read but me and I'd like to stop going to school."

"Going to school is the law," my mother said. "You have to go to school and learn to read."

"I'd rather be a waitress or work at a pet store. I'd even rather wash dishes than go to school."

"You'll learn to read and then you'll forget that you ever had a problem," my mother said.

But so far, she had been wrong.

I've been in the cubicle for so long that I'm beginning to get sleepy. It's very difficult to sleep with your feet resting on the toilet paper holder and your bottom on the toilet seat. The trouble with the toilet seats in our girls' room is they have no tops, so you can't close them. You can imagine how uncomfortable I am. And hungry. I'm thinking about chocolate mousse cake, which is my favorite, and fried chicken and mashed potatoes with butter melting, when I suddenly hear the thunder of footsteps outside the door, which means it's time for lunch. Certainly someone will have to come into the girls' room now, I think. And I'm right.

I hear the squeak of the door and giggling.

"Did you see the way Ms. Burke turned purple when Zale left the classroom?"

I recognize the voice. It is Ana Castillo and she's my friend. She's from Puerto Rico and is just learning English, so she has trouble with reading too.

"I don't blame Zale," the other girl says. I don't recognize her voice. "Ms. Burke is mean. She wrote a letter to my parents to tell them I didn't try hard enough to learn to read and I should go to another school."

"Me too," Ana says.

"So what are you going to do?"

"My mother has a fire temper and she screamed at Ms. Burke that she was the teacher and her job was to teach me to read."

"I wish my mother had a fire temper. She just gets mad at me," the other girl says.

I'm thinking about my mother. She doesn't have a fire temper and she doesn't get mad at me and she doesn't get mad at the school because I don't know how to read. She gets mad at other things. At my father, at my grandmother when she whines about her hard life, at me when my room is messy or I forget to change the kitty litter box for Bewilder, my yellow-and-white kitten that I got for Christmas. But she doesn't get mad often and mostly as I've told Esmeralda, she's a No-Fuss Good-Time mom who says what she thinks.

She thinks I'm too stubborn. She told me that the other day.

We were in the kitchen and she was making gnocchi from scratch and I was supposed to be reading aloud to her but I'd quit.

"What do you mean too stubborn?" I asked.

"Stubborn is good," my mother said. "It means you think for yourself and don't follow the leader and that's good."

"So?" I asked.

"Too stubborn means you dig your heels into the dirt and won't move even if a giant snowplow is about to run over you."

"We don't have snowplows here."

"You know what I mean, Zale," my mother said, dropping the gnocchi in boiling water. "If you decide you're not going to do something—eat dinner, brush your teeth, go to a birthday party, learn to read, you won't budge."

"What you don't understand is that it's hard being the stupidest person in the class," I said. "Sometimes I don't even want to try."

"You're not the stupidest person in the class and so what if you were. Many of the kids have worse problems."

"Not that I know about," I said, shredding the Parmesan cheese with our new shredder. "Anyway, it's embarrassing if you can't read. I'd rather work in a filling station."

The truth is I know that the kids in Special Reading with Ms. Burke don't know how to read either. That some of them may even be worse than I am. My mother tells me all the time.

"There are plenty of children who don't know how to read, so don't feel bad about it. It isn't a big deal because it's a deal you can change."

The trouble is, when I'm at school, I feel as if I'm the only one.

Ana says she's ready to go to lunch and I hear the door open, so I lean down to peek under the cubicle, and I recognize Sasha's blue socks with white kittens. Sasha Miller. I can hardly believe it. I thought Sasha was the best student in Special Reading. She always finishes the chapter books. She knows the answers to all the questions and raises her hand in class, which I never do, and can even read aloud without tripping over the words, which happens to me every time I read out loud. "P-p-p-peony B-b-b-blue-fi-sh"

"Nerves," my mother tells me. "You never stutter at home."

I'm just about to stand on the toilet seat to see if I can look over the cubicle, when the door opens again and I know it's Ms. Burke.

"Zale?" she calls. I can see her feet. She's wearing low-heeled black shoes and someone is with her, also a grown-up, in boots.

"Zale, are you here?" She's looking under the cubicles. I can tell by listening to her heels click and stop and click and stop.

"Not here," she says.

The water turns on, so I suppose she is washing her hands.

"Do you think she might have gone home?" another voice says, and I recognize the voice of Ms. Peach, the principal. I like Ms. Peach. She has always been nice to me and she's funny and good-tempered even with the boys.

"I can't imagine Zale would just go home in the

middle of the day without telling anyone. Very nervy."

I never thought of going home, but it pleases me that they think I might. I'd be afraid to walk down Park Road by myself. My house is across the highway, which my mother won't let me cross without a policeman. Besides, I wouldn't want to spend all day at home while my mother is at work, even with Bewilder. She's only a cat. She doesn't talk.

"Did you check the lunchroom?" Ms. Peach says.

"I will." She turns off the water. "She just walked right out of the classroom when I told her she couldn't be excused," Ms. Burke says.

"She must have been upset."

"She should be. She doesn't do her homework."

"Well, check the lunchroom," Ms. Peach says.

"I will," Ms. Burke replies. "And I'll send someone to check the playground."

"And if we don't find her, we're going to have to call her mother right away," Ms. Peach says.

I don't want anyone to call my mother.

I wrap my arms around my knees and press my forehead against them. It's cold here. I'm only wearing a long-sleeve T-shirt and jeans and I need a sweater. Probably if I don't eat lunch soon, I'll faint.

That's what my mother says will happen to her if she doesn't eat.

My plan has been to stay in this cubicle until the end of school, wait until most of the students have left the building to go home or to tutoring or piano lessons or the dentist, and then to slip out of the girls' room, down the back steps, out the playground door, and home.

But if they're calling my mother, I can't.

She will be so worried. I think about her at the supermarket standing at the checkout register in her blue uniform with *Mary Alice* embroidered on the pocket, and she is smiling at everyone, telling them hello, asking about their children, handing the babies a cookie from the box of animal crackers she keeps beside her at the register.

My mother is almost always cheerful, and it isn't easy. She works all day and sometimes people get angry at her because their carton of milk has a hole in it or the nuts fall out of the almond bag or the lettuce is brown at the edges. And she is always pleasant even though it isn't her fault.

"I'm not responsible for lettuce," she'll tell me. "Only the cash register."

Thinking about my mother just now has started me thinking about myself. I'm sitting here shivering, wishing I had my peanut butter sandwich and a sweater and that the bell for dismissal was ringing and I start to wonder whether reading is easier than I think it is. Maybe I haven't been trying hard enough, I think. Maybe I can learn if I don't call Esmerelda when I get home from school this afternoon. Maybe I won't turn on the television. At least Mom made a new batch of chocolate chip cookies to eat while I'm trying to read *Peony Bluefish and the Bag Lady*.

I didn't wear my watch today but it's probably late and Ms. Burke has gone to the lunchroom and I won't be there. Then she'll ask the kids in my class whether they've seen me and they'll say no and someone will check the playground and I won't be there. Ms. Burke will march to Ms. Peach's office to tell her that I have officially disappeared. Then Ms. Peach will call my mother and my mother will go crazy.

I have to get out of here without being seen.

My plan is to slip out now, head down the back steps, past the kindergarten and first grade, go out the side door, and run to the supermarket so I can get there before Ms. Peach makes her telephone call.

But as I'm thinking about a new plan, the door to the girls' room opens and I see four shoes passing beside my cubicle. I wait. Someone is crying.

"I read the whole first chapter twice," the crying girl says. "I can only read about half the words."

"Ms. Burke knows you're trying," another girl says.

I recognize the voice of Jilly O'Shee, who sits next to me in homeroom. She isn't in Special Reading with us, but she doesn't tease us either like some of the girls in the fourth grade do.

"She called my mother and told her I was only a little better in reading and by now I should be much better."

Very quietly I lift the hook on the door.

"So what happened today?" Jilly asks.

"I was telling about my parents going to India and then Ms. Burke asked me a question and I didn't know the answer. And then she asked another question and then I cried. She told me I had lots of time to read the chapter and I should know everything."

I put my feet on the ground and stand up.

It is Betsy Ford. I can hardly believe my ears. Perfect Betsy Ford with her high ponytail and Big Personality.

I push open the door and in the mirror over the sinks, I see Betsy Ford's tear-streaked face dripping with water because she has just washed it.

"Hi," I say.

"Zale," Jilly says. "Ms. Burke was just in the lunchroom looking for you."

"I was here," I say, standing next to Betsy and washing my face.

"In the girls' room?"

"I've been here since I left reading."

Betsy looks over at me. "For almost two hours? What did you do?"

"Nothing," I say. "I came in here because I didn't want to listen to Ms. Burke complain about me anymore."

Betsy smiles at me through her tears, and I smile back.

"Me too," Betsy says. "She calls my parents and tells them I don't try."

"Me too."

"Do you try?"

I hesitate before I answer.

"Maybe not so much," I say. "I watch television until my mom gets home from work."

"I do too," Betsy Ford says.

"I've had trouble ever since first grade and sometimes I think I'm afraid to try." It's the first time I've ever told anyone at school the truth, and I'm surprised at how easy it is to tell Betsy Ford, who was my enemy only a couple of hours ago. "It's like if you work very hard and still can't learn to read, you must be stupid."

"Exactly." She throws her arm around my shoulder. "Did you have lunch yet?"

"Not yet," I say. "I've been here all morning and now I'm starving."

"Well, let's sit at the same table," Betsy says.

"Great," I say. "I'll meet you in the lunchroom, but first I have to tell Ms. Peach I've been found."

"We'll save you a seat," Jilly says, waving as I head off to Ms. Peach's office.

I stop at my locker and pick up my lunch, slipping the chocolate chip cookie out of the bag, eating it on the way.

Tonight, I'm thinking, when my mother gets home from the supermarket, I'll be sitting at the kitchen table reading *Peony Bluefish and the Bag Lady* and she'll ask me what I've been doing.

"Just reading," I'll say. Maybe I'll finish the first two chapters by the time she gets home. Maybe I'll be able to answer all the questions tomorrow in Special Reading.

"Have you been watching television, Zale?" she'll ask. "Or talking to Esmerelda on the telephone?"

"No," I'll say. "I haven't."

Which will be the truth.

Susan Shreve's School Report

Favorite Class: Art
Least Favorite Class: Math
Best Teacher Ever: Miss Hardell, fourth grade
Worst Smell at School: Cafeteria
Favorite Cafeteria Meal: Chocolate pudding
Meanest Thing Someone Ever Did to Me: Thumbtacks on my desk chair
The best time in gym was when: it was over.
Best Field Trip Ever Taken: Train to New York City. I liked the train part better than the museums.
Best Memory: Hiding in the bushes with my friends when recess was over
Some of the books I've written are: *The Flunking of Joshua T. Bates; Joshua T. Bates Takes Charge; Joshua T. Bates in Trouble Again; Blister; Jonah the Whale; Ghost Cats; Goodbye, Amanda the Good;* and several other books for adults.

TIED TO ZELDA

by David Rice

My next-door neighbor, Zelda Fuerte, scares me and gives me the chills at the same time. She is the biggest tomboy in town and the evil twin sister I never wanted. She can outrun any boy, climb a tree faster than a cat, and spit the farthest. My dad always invites her to our house to play, since she doesn't have a father around. She's the son my father wants me to be. He always says, "Do it like Zelda." When my dad isn't around, Zelda likes to play "Tie Up," a game she invented. She is always tying me up, but I always escape.

The only time I am safe is summer. That's when Zelda, her mother, and sisters drive to Utah to pick fruit. My father and I help Zelda and her family board up their house and load their van. Zelda always looks a little sad when she leaves, and I am too, since I have to mow their lawn while they are away. In the fall, I only see Zelda in the school halls and we exchange semi-friendly "Hi's." Other than that, I stay far away from her.

Our school has a yearly tradition called Sadie Hawkins' Day, where boys and girls are paired up to compete in a three-legged race and an egg-tossing contest. I think it sounds kind of dumb, but there *are* big prizes worth big bucks. If you win the three-legged race, you get two passes to Splash World for the whole summer and free hot dogs. That's pretty cool. If you win the egg-tossing contest, you get two passes to sports camp at the local college. Three weeks of running and sweating and the whole time coaches yelling? No thanks.

Anyway, one week before Sadie Hawkins' Day, the teachers got all the fifth graders into the cafeteria and they brought out two big baskets, one with the boys' names and the other with the girls' names. Our drama teacher spun the baskets around a few times and took a name from each basket. He was really hamming it up. "Now hear this, now hear this," he said over a megaphone. Then he called a girl's name real slowly, and there was an "Oooooooooooo" throughout the cafeteria. Then he called out a boy's name and everyone cheered, whistled, and clapped. The next girl's name he pulled out was "Zeeellllda Fuerte!" That's how he called everyone's name. When her name was called out, my best friend Jorge leaned over to me.

"Man, whoever is Zelda's partner will win both contests," he said.

"Phffffft, forget it. I don't want to go to sports camp," I said.

"Don't you want the Splash World pass?" Jorge asked. "Free admission for the whole summer and free hot dogs too."

"Yeah, it'd be cool, but I don't want to be tied up to Zelda," I said.

"What's wrong with being tied up to Zelda?" Jorge asked.

"She's a knot nazi," I said.

Our teacher pulled out a boy's name and held it high. He smiled and pointed at me like he was a game show host. "Alllfoooooonso Flores!"

Jorge and the whole cafeteria started laughing. I looked over at Zelda, and she threw her arms up like she lost the national championship. After all the names were called, Zelda walked up to me.

"Alfonso, after school, meet me in the gym," she said.

"But I have a computer club meeting and I'm—" I tried to finish, but she cut me off.

"After school, in the gym. Don't make me come looking for you. I know where you live." She spun around and walked off in a huff.

After school, during the computer club meeting, Jorge asked me if he could borrow my Splash World pass.

"Look, I don't want to be tied up, and I don't want to throw eggs," I said.

"C'mon, don't be a baby. It's just your ankles tied together, and everybody likes throwing eggs," Jorge said. "And if you win, we can share Splash World and hot dogs."

"Well, if you want the passes so bad, why don't you and your partner practice, and you can win the passes to Splash World."

"Because Zelda's the best. No one can beat her," Jorge said.

Then the door busted open. And there was Zelda

161

looking really mad. My first thought was to run, but she was blocking the only escape route.

"I told you to be in the gym after school so we could practice," she shouted firmly.

"Umm, can't you find someone else?" I squeaked.

"I can't, you know the rules. Monday we'll practice. We're going to win," she said, and slammed the door.

Jorge threw his arms up like he won a gold medal. "Splash World, here we come."

I was a little worried, but the weekend was here, and I thought Zelda would forget, but she didn't. On Sunday night she came to my house, and my mom let her in. I was helping my father tighten a nut under the bathroom sink, unaware that Zelda was working on my mother. My dad told me to get him a glass of water, and when I walked into the kitchen, they were sitting at the breakfast table, and Mom looked thrilled. She waved a friendly dishrag at me.

"You didn't tell me you and Zelda were partners in the Sadie Hawkins' Day festival."

"But I don't—" I managed to say, then Zelda cut me off.

"If we win the three-legged race, we get two passes to Splash World, and if we win the egg-tossing contest, we get two passes to summer sports camp. Isn't that great?" Zelda said, all happy.

My mother shook her excited dishrag. "Wow, when is the festival? I mean, you two need to practice."

It was exactly what Zelda wanted to hear. "That's why I came by," she said. "The festival is this Friday, and we need to practice every day after school."

"Phffffft, forget it," I said. "I don't want to go to sports camp."

My mother turned to me, narrowed her eyes, and shook her angry dishrag. "Whatever. You're going to be partners with Zelda."

Zelda smirked at me, and when my mother turned back to her, she looked all hurt and sad. Zelda sighed, "Well, Mrs. Flores, if Alfonso doesn't want to be my partner, I guess I'll have to find someone else." And she lowered her head.

My mother tossed the emotionally wrecked dishrag on the table. Then my father walked in with a wrench in his hand and put it down on the table with a hard metal sound. "What do you mean you don't want to be Zelda's partner?"

"But, Dad, I don't want to go to sports camp," I said.

He picked up his wrench and waved it like a warlock ready to cast a spell. "Alfonso, you're going to practice every day with Zelda. All you ever do is play on your computer. If you don't practice, you'll find your computer in the trash can," Dad said, and tossed his wrench on the kitchen table.

Zelda threw her arms up in glee. "Great. We'll practice every day till we get it right."

My mother smiled and picked up the happy dishrag and waved it. "Practice makes perfect."

I dropped my head in defeat.

In the morning I cautiously walked the school halls. Turning corners slowly, trying to avoid Zelda. Then I saw her marching toward me. She yelled, "Freeze." I took a step back and saw the boys' rest room and thought about running in there, but when I turned, there was Monica, Zelda's best friend. I took another step back and felt a heavy hand on my shoulder. I turned around, and there stood Zelda.

"Where do you think you're going?" Zelda asked.

"I have to pee really bad," I said.

Zelda pushed me against the lockers.

"Squeeze your legs and hold it," she said.

Then Zelda poked my chest with each word as she said, "Today, after school. You better be there."

Monica poked my chest too. "You better. We want the sports passes," she said.

I was scared, but then I saw Jorge coming down the hall. I shouted, "Help me!" I felt better when Jorge walked up, but then he and Zelda acted like they were best friends.

"What's up?" Jorge said to Zelda.

"Just making sure Alfonso meets me after school."

"He'll be there. We want the passes to Splash World," Jorge said as he crossed his arms.

"But I don't want to play Tie Up." I pleaded.

Jorge looked confused. "Tie Up?" he said.

Zelda poked my chest. "You better play Tie Up, or else." She paused and grinned. "I'll tell your father and he'll take away your computer."

I looked at Jorge for help. "Quit acting like a baby," he said. "Everybody likes being tied up and throwing eggs."

After school Zelda escorted me outside to the

recess area. She put down her backpack and took out a piece of rope. "I always carry my own rope," she said as she raised her eyebrows a couple of times. Fear swelled in my stomach. Zelda tied my ankle to hers real tight and I felt my bones crushing. She said we had to run like one person. We started running, but I tripped and made us fall. She shook her head and pulled me up. I thought for sure she was going to beat me up, but instead she smiled.

"You okay?" she asked.

I nodded as I brushed off my jeans.

Monica and two other girls cheered us on.

"C'mon, Alfonso, you can do it!"

They shouted like cheerleaders. I never had anyone cheer for me, and it felt good. Zelda put her arm around my waist, and I put my arm around her shoulders. She said to hold her tight.

"Okay," she said. "We start off slow until we're together, and then we speed it up."

We took small slow steps and then faster, bigger ones, and then we were running. Zelda's friends were cheering louder and I felt like a sports star. We slowed down to a stop, and turned around and started all over again. We ran back and forth, and each time we were getting faster and faster. Then we fell again, but this time we fell hard. I banged my head against the ground and got a nasty red mark, but no blood. Zelda and her friends helped me up. They had their hands all over me, brushing off the dry grass and fixing my hair, asking me if I was okay and stuff like that. Then Zelda brought out a golf ball.

"Time to practice egg tossing." She raised the white ball to my eyes. "Use both hands and keep your eyes on the ball."

We started at five feet from each other and tossed the ball back and forth. Each time I dropped the ball, we started all over again, and she'd say, "Only the ball," but it was hard for me to see the white blurry object. She'd toss the ball, and I'd lose it in the clouds. Maybe I needed glasses. Each time I dropped the ball, I thought Zelda was going to get mad, but she didn't.

"This is practice. You can mess up all you want, but not on game day," she said.

I nodded. "Right, Coach," I said.

She smiled and punched my arm.

I found out that other teams were practicing—

even Jorge was practicing with his partner, and that got me pumped. It made me want to win the race and the contest. Zelda and I could run the three-legged race really fast, and I was getting better at catching the ball. The second it touched my fingers, I closed my hands tightly around it. I could tell Zelda was proud of me.

The night before the festival, Zelda came over to my house with a bag of pan dulce.

"What's this?" I asked.

"I got you some heart-shaped cookies and mar-ranitos. I think people should be rewarded for their hard work."

She smiled and put the bag out, and I was about to take it. Then I noticed she was looking around me and she whispered in a sneaky tone, "Who's here?"

"Nobody, my parents—"

She cut me off and snatched the bag away and began poking me in the chest with her stiff finger and raised her voice. "Tomorrow, I want to win." Her face was inches from mine.

I backed up. "Hey, I'll do my best."

"You better. If you don't, I'm tying you up to a tree in the middle of nowhere and letting the ants eat you."

"Look, what's the big deal? It's just a stupid contest," I said, shrugging my shoulders.

"I want the passes to sports camp," she said in a deep voice, and lowered her head like a charging bull.

"But who wants to spend three weeks at a sports camp?" I said.

"I do," she said. "I'd rather be at sports camp than in Utah with my jerk father."

I knew her parents were separated, but I thought her father lived in a nearby town.

"I thought your father lived in the Valley."

Zelda shook her head and let out a deep sigh. "No, he lives in Utah and we have to stay with him and my tío. They're both jerks. All they do is drink beer and smoke all night."

"Can't you stay somewhere else?"

"No—think we're rich or something? I want me and my mom and sisters to stay here for the summer. If I get the sports passes, my mom said we'd stay and she'd find a job here."

"Well, if we win the three-legged race, can't you trade your Splash World pass with someone for the sports camp pass?" I asked.

"No, I promised my mother I'd let my little sisters

have the Splash World pass if I won it." Her eyes got all watery. "Don't you see? We have to win the egg toss. I don't want my mother to be around my father."

She dropped her head and let out a sigh. She held out the bag of pan dulce, and I took it.

She sniffed a little and looked up at me. "Just do your best, okay?"

I nodded. "I promise," I said.

The next day when I walked to the recess area, there was lots going on. The high school conjunto band was playing, and there was a popcorn machine, chili frito pies, fajita tacos, buttered elotes, and raspas in all flavors. The sports camp had a banner up, and so did Splash World. There were kids tied at the ankles walking around and others on the ground all tangled up. I felt a tap on my shoulder and turned around, and there was Zelda. She didn't waste any time. She gave me a high five and tied our ankles together, and we walked around the recess area like one big person.

There was a long line of three-legged kids for the three-legged race, but Zelda said to focus on the finish line, not the competition. I was a little jumpy when we got in our starting positions, but Zelda put her arm around me and we held each other tight. I heard a whistle blow, and we were flying. I could hear our hearts pounding when we crossed the finish line, but we couldn't stop. We tripped all over the place and hit the ground rolling.

But it was worth it because we won first place. Zelda and I were on the ground laughing through our bruises, and Jorge came running over to us.

"Splash World, oh yeah," he said.

Zelda and I walked around trying to shake off our scraped elbows and knees. Kids I didn't know were walking up to us saying what a great job we did.

The egg toss had even more kids than the three-legged race. The teachers placed a long white string across the ground to divide the teams. Zelda put her hand up to give me another high five. Two teachers walked between the teams carrying cartons of twenty-four eggs. When the teachers walked up to us, they asked who was going to choose the egg. I pointed to Zelda.

Zelda took one egg and held it with her fingers. She moved her wrist back and forth, studying the egg, looking for little thin cracks. She put it back and took another one. The teachers were like: "We don't have all day." Zelda held that egg and studied it too and let the weight of it move her arm up and down. She raised it up to my eye level. "Only the ball," she said.

The rules were easy. The kids on the right of our drama teacher threw first. Each time you caught the egg, you'd take one step back. Getting farther and farther apart. The last team left, without breaking their egg, won the contest.

When the whistle blew, all the kids threw their eggs except Zelda. She waited, and I could hear kids dropping their eggs and lots of laughing. I turned to look, but Zelda shouted, "Hey, focus on me and the egg."

I nodded. She tossed her egg with a nice gentle arch, and I put my hands together and caught it easily, but we were only five feet from each other. We took a step back, and the whistle blew. Zelda put her hands up and gestured for me to wait until the other kids threw theirs. Through my side vision I could see eggs all over the sky, I heard eggs breaking and kids screaming "Ahhhhhh" and "Yuck," but Zelda kept gesturing for me to look at her.

172

After a few seconds she nodded, and I tossed my egg. She caught it like it belonged to her. Toss after toss I could hear more eggs breaking and the crowd laughing, but I kept my eyes on Zelda. Finally we were really far from each other, and there were only three teams left.

Then the teachers brought us closer and made us put our arms out so we could touch fingertips with the kids on each side. The whistle blew, but none of the kids threw their eggs. I looked to the right of Zelda, and there was Jorge waving.

Our drama teacher shouted through his megaphone, "Wellllll, somebody throw an egg."

We didn't say anything for a moment, and then Zelda spoke up.

"We'll throw first," she said. The crowd went "Ooooooooo." I looked at Zelda, and she walked up to me.

"Do your best." She handed me the egg. Then she ran back to her position and nodded at me. I took a few deep breaths and threw the egg with all my strength. The egg had a high arch. I overthrew it. Zelda had to take several quick steps back and dove for the egg. I put my hands to my face ready to scream, but Zelda was a super athlete. The egg disappeared into her body, and she rolled on the ground and jumped up with the egg safe in her hand. The crowd went wild.

The next team threw their egg, but the boy threw way too short. The girl ran forward fast and caught it, but the egg exploded in her hands and face. The crowd went "Eeeeeelooooooooooo," and there was tons of laughter. After the crowd settled down, Jorge threw his egg, and it was perfect. His partner didn't have to move an inch, and it floated right into her hands. The crowd cheered and clapped like a bunch of excited monkeys.

Our drama teacher put his hand up. "Okay, now both teams must throw at the same time."

The crowd went wild again.

We all took a step back, and Zelda was so far away, she was a blur. I looked at Jorge and back at Zelda, and I put my hands up in a time-out gesture like they do in sports games. "Time out," I shouted.

I heard the crowd yelling, "Hey, you can't do that! Hurry up, throw it!" I ran to the middle of the field and gestured for Jorge to meet me. He ran to me.

"What's up?" he said.

"Listen, I don't think I can catch the egg. I can't see anything," I said. "Let's make a deal. If you catch the egg, you give me your pass to sports camp, and I'll give you my pass to Splash World."

I could tell he wasn't going for it, so I added more. "And I'll loan you any video game I have for a whole month."

Jorge rolled his eyes. "Phfffft, only one?"

"Okay, two," I said.

Jorge put his hand on his chin and lightly stroked it. "Yeah, but what if you do catch the egg?"

"Then I'll give you my pass to Splash World and my pass to sports camp."

"And the video games?" Jorge grinned.

"Yes, yes. You can still borrow them."

Jorge put out his hand, and we shook on it. "It's a deal," he said.

I ran back to my position and rubbed my sweaty palms on my shirt and nodded.

Zelda took a step back and threw the egg like a football. It was a perfect spiral. But it was going too fast. I had to step back and just as it touched my hands, I tripped over my feet. The egg went through my hands and hit me square on the forehead. There was egg all over me, and I wiped my face and looked at Jorge, who was laughing like a nut with his egg in his hand, jumping up and down, like a freaked out kangaroo. "Splash World and hot dogs!" he kept shouting.

He jumped over to Zelda, and I could tell he was telling her the deal I made with him, and she began jumping up and down and ran toward me. She gave me a high five and punched my arm. She put her arm around my shoulders, and I put my arm around hers and we walked without being tied together.

That night my parents came to my room and knocked on the door frame.

"Hey m'ijo, Zelda's mother just called and told us what you did today. Your mother and I are very proud of you," Dad said.

"Thanks," I said.

"Listen, tomorrow we're going to buy you a summer pass for Splash World. Sound good to you?" Dad said, and Mom nodded happily.

I thought for a moment. "Thanks, Dad, thanks, Mom, but I'd rather go to sports camp."

They looked a little confused. "But we thought you wanted to go to Splash World," Mom said.

"Well, yeah, but Zelda is going to sports camp, and she might need a partner," I said.

David Rice's School Report

Favorite Class: Science. I wanted to build a rocket ship.

Least Favorite Class: I liked all my classes.

Best Teacher Ever: In school, Mrs. Teri Zavaleta

Worst Smell at School: The boys' rest room. Toilets never flushed right.

Favorite Cafeteria Food: Enchiladas

Meanest Thing Someone Ever Did to Me: Nothing, really. I was the prankster...

Best Prank Ever Played: Catching tiny bugs and putting them in straws and shooting them in kids' hair

Best Field Trip Taken: The Buttercrust Bakery. We each got a small loaf of bread and a baker's hat.

Best Memory: My tío dated the lunch lady, Rosie. And so Rosie always gave me a big scoop of ice cream. Then my tío broke up with Rosie and from then on, none of the lunch ladies gave me ice cream.

Some of the books I've written are: *Crazy Loco* (which was chosen as an ALA Best Book for YA) and *Give a Pig a Chance,* both of which are short-story collections.

Grade

knowl-

ORMANCE
TH

nt

ardy

's Comment: (please check)

ied with report ......

re conference ......

gnature of Parent or Guardian:

st Quarter

Quarter